WILLIAM MCGUIRE

Missing

Missing: It should have been a dream vacation but instead it was the holiday from hell.

ACKNOWLEDGEMENT

For my family.

For my friends.

For myself.

My thanks to my team of readers who told me the truth.

My special thanks to two people who shared their valuable time and knowledge with me during the writing of this book: Anne, my sister and computer expert, and Sandy, my long-suffering and workaholic agent. (Rolling Thunder)

PROLOGUE

"Would you like a doughnut?" Louise asked David.

David didn't hear her. He was too engrossed in his James Patterson novel 'Cross'. Patterson was his favourite author and he was half way through his book, on the last day of his holiday, and nothing was going to stop him from finishing it. At least, that's what he kept telling himself, but something wasn't right.

They were sitting in the hotel reception area on bright orange sofas, which looked both modern and retro at the same time. Guests were checking in and out at regular intervals, but it seemed so peaceful. No noise. David thought that strange. Very strange.

He really didn't want to go home. He didn't want their holiday to end. They were due to leave Barcelona on the 10-15 pm flight to Glasgow, but he didn't know if they would make that plane.

He was certainly dressed for travel, in his lived-in Levis and soft touch Adidas polo shirt. On his feet he wore the only pair of shoes which he had left, (his other pair had been stolen). Louise hated them! She called them his 'old man shoes', because she reckoned they were the type of shoes that old men wore and David was only in his early fifties. In her mind, she thought he wore those jeans and shoes just to annoy her, but the fact of the matter was that he just felt really relaxed in this get-up.

Well he usually did, but not today.

"Would you like a doughnut?" Louise asked again, taking the purse from her large beige handbag.

They had found a great little bakery right next to their hotel the previous morning where the doughnuts were freshly made, and they were to die for.

Then it hit him. He knew why he felt so tense.

"No thanks, I'm back on my diet, and anyway, I've had two already today. Come to that, so have you!"

He tried not to show the tension in his voice.

"I know," said Louise "but they're so good and I'm still on holiday, even if you say your holiday's over!"

Louise got up and walked over to the large revolving door drawing admiring looks from the bellboy and the concierge, with her tight jeans and blond hair. She smiled back at David and pushed her way through the doors. She looked very cool. Very calm.

'This is it' he thought to himself. He had waited three years for this moment. Now it was here, he didn't know what to do. All he knew for sure was that his wife was going to disappear, and he had to just sit there. He had to let it happen.

As he looked out of the massive window, it made him think of the Alfred Hitchcock film 'Rear Window', in which James Stewart plays a man recovering from a broken leg. He can only sit and look out of his window. He can watch, but he can't do. David felt a bit like that, although he didn't have a broken leg.

Louise appeared to his left. She waved at him and then moved her hand to her mouth, pretending she was eating a doughnut. She seemed to walk in slow motion. Then she smiled one last time just before she disappeared.

David just sat there sweating in the realisation that he might never see his wife again.

But he knew that's the way it had to be.

For now anyway.

Part 1

Chapter 1

Barcelona, Valletta, Naples, Livorno, Rome, Cannes and Barcelona again - what an itinerary!

David Telfer had finally found the cruise his wife wanted. She'd been very specific with her instructions, but he had done it.

"Louise" he shouted. "I think I've found it."

A picture of the cruise ship, The American Gem, filled the laptop screen, just waiting for Louise's approval.

Seconds later she appeared at his left shoulder.

"Oh my God, it looks awesome" she cried out, as he read out the ports of call.

"That's it. That's the holiday I want."

"I haven't found a hotel or booked the flights yet. I'll try and sort them out first before I book the cruise" added David.

"Great. You book everything else, but don't book the hotel. I want to pick that."

"What? You usually leave that sort of thing up to me."

"Well not this time. I'll choose the hotel. Right, I'll go and put the kettle on" she said, as she made her way through to the kitchen.

David immediately set about finding the flights. It only took him five minutes. He then tried to find a hotel in Barcelona. He found one situated in the heart of Las Ramblas...superb location.

'She's got to love this one' he thought to himself as he called Louise.

"The flights are booked. Do you want to take a look at this hotel?"

She rushed into the living room.

"I told you, I want to choose the hotel" she shouted.

"All right, keep your hair on. At least have a look at this one." It surprised him how angry she was. She handed David his tea, in his usual mug. 'I'M THE BOSS' was scrawled across the side in big letters. Just below it said, (at least he thinks he is). Louise sat down at the laptop and sipped her tea. She had a china cup. She didn't do mugs.

Seconds later she spoke. "That one."

"That was quick" answered a shocked David.

She had picked out the Hotel Sants.

He was impressed by the reviews. Every reviewer said they would go back to the hotel. It was a great location, as it was situated near to the Sants railway-metro station, the main station in Barcelona, and 'therefore easily accessible from the airport' as one of the reviews put it. It also had a swimming pool on the roof. That sealed it for him.

"Well? What do you think?"

"I think it's great, but how did you find it so quickly?"

Louise didn't answer him. She rose from the chair.

"Let's go out and celebrate. You finalise the booking, and I'll go and get changed."

At that she left the room.

David sat all alone, staring at the computer screen, pleased but puzzled. Questions streamed into his mind. Since her illness Louise had found it very difficult to make even the simplest of decisions, so why had she been so insistent on choosing the hotel? Why had she been so angry with him when he had tried to show her the hotel he had picked? That just wasn't like her. He cast those questions to the back of his mind.

One other thought troubled him.

On reading all the reviews about the hotel and Barcelona itself, every single one of them ended with the same warning.

Beware of pickpockets!

Watch your luggage!

Ladies, keep hold of your handbag!
Always keep hold of your hand luggage!
David would soon wish that he had taken more heed
of this last piece of advice.

Chapter 2

It was the 6th of September and David and Louise were in Barcelona on a hot and sunny Sunday morning. Their journey the previous day had been straightforward apart from the two-hour delay at Cardiff airport. However that didn't inconvenience them in any way because their cruise ship didn't leave until Sunday, and they had the whole night to spend in Barcelona. In fact if the truth be told, they actually enjoyed sitting at the bar in Cardiff's departure lounge having a few extra drinks, and just chilling out. David had a couple of vodkas and diet coke, while Louise had decided to try a new drink (for her anyway), that being gin and bitter lemon. Someone had told her that it was a nice drink, but it was thought to make anyone drinking it feel depressed. After another four gin and bitter lemons she decided that it was a lovely drink. As for making you feel depressed, she thought that was hogwash. Indeed anyone watching Louise laughing and joking with David while they were having a good old Scottish blether would have had to agree with her.

Their plan was to leave their hotel at about twelve noon, as they wouldn't be allowed to board their ship before this time. David woke up at 10 am. He decided he would go for a walk and find out how far the hotel was from the port, so he shaved, showered, and then dressed. He put the clothes in which he had travelled, into his new hand luggage bag, along with the mobile phone chargers. In the front zipped compartment, he placed the documents required to board the ship, the tickets for their flight home, and the tickets for their two day stay at the hotel- post cruise, all of which Louise would normally keep in her hand bag......but not today.

As they were in a room on the fifth floor, 507, he decided to take the lift down to reception rather than walk down all those stairs. There, he asked how much it would cost in a taxi to go to the port. The receptionist lifted her head from her computer screen and answered,

"No more than ten euros. It's not very far."

A look of sheer surprise spread across David's face.

"It can't be, can it?" He glanced at the name tag attached to the lady's pristine gleaming white blouse, and read the name aloud.

"Maria Lopez! When did you start working in this hotel?"

David had met Maria when he'd been in Barcelona seven years previously, while attending a confectionery buyer's conference. It had taken place in another city hotel, where Maria had been working at the time, and she had helped him with various problems he had encountered that week. With many years experience in the hotel trade Maria had developed a great memory for faces and after only one clue from David, she recognised him.

"Confectionery buyer's conference, seven years ago in the Hotel Presidente" prompted David.

"David Telfer. It's so nice to see you again. Are you here for pleasure?" she said with a glint in her eye, "or business?" she added. She was genuinely pleased to see him again.

"Pleasure this time Maria, so I don't expect to have many problems to solve this week. By the way you haven't changed a bit."

"You also David, that is why I recognised you so quickly" she replied in her sexy Spanish accent.

"Thanks Maria, I hope you mean that and you're not just humouring me."

They both smiled.

"My wife and I are going on a cruise this afternoon, but we're staying here for two nights post cruise. Maybe we can have a chat then, and I'll introduce you to Louise" said David as he made his way towards the hotel revolving doors.

"That would be nice. Just in case I don't see you before you go, enjoy your cruise. Adios."

As soon as David was outside he felt the real heat of the sun, it was very warm. He also noticed that there was a taxi parked at the rank just outside the hotel. Reminding himself what Maria had said, 'ten euros to the port', he decided to ask the driver the same question.

"How much would it cost to take me to the port?"

The driver extended both arms out to each side of his body, palms facing upwards. He shrugged his shoulders in that typical Spanish manner.

"Mmmm..... twenty five euros."

"Typical. Taxi drivers must be the same the world over."

David walked away, shaking his head.

He then went for a stroll around the local area, just to get the feel of the place. That's what he loved to do. To walk the streets all by himself, taking in the noises, the smells and the vibes of a bustling city. He really loved the vibes he was getting from Barcelona. So much so that he forgot the time, and only realised on looking at his watch, that it was ten past twelve.

He made his way back to the hotel.

When he reached the room Louise was ready and waiting.

"Is it as warm as it looks outside?" she asked.

"Warm? It's absolutely glorious," answered David. "Shall we cruise?" he added, with a grin that stretched from ear to ear. Louise just smiled and grabbed her suitcase. He followed with his case and small hand luggage bag.

After checking out of the hotel they went to the taxi rank just outside. The street was quiet. No taxis. Louise headed for the shade of the hotel awning, while David basked in the sun, still clutching his small bag. A couple of minutes later, he sat it down beside the two other cases, next to Louise. He walked twenty yards up to the end of the street where the main road passed by the side of the hotel. He thought it might be easier to flag down a car there, however there were no taxis to be seen. He then walked back to the kerb, to make sure they would at least be first in the queue. A minute later a young man suddenly appeared at his right hand side and asked him something in Spanish. David could only make out the words 'Place d'Espagna'.

"No hablar Espagnol", he answered, feeling proud of himself that the man seemed to have understood his reply. The young man mumbled something else in Spanish and then leapt into a car that had just drawn up at the kerb. As it sped off into the distance David turned round to speak to Louise, only to see her in sheer panic and screaming at him,

"David, your bag's gone!"

Chapter 3

David and Louise were both rooted to the spot. Neither of them had ever had anything stolen from them before. Louise, knowing that the tickets were in the bag, shouted over to David,

"Will we be allowed to board the ship?"

David couldn't think straight but answered anyway. "Yes, don't worry about that."

He started running down the road where the car had gone, turning round to Louise and shouting, "Stay there, I'll be back in five minutes." He was hoping that he would find his bag lying in the street, having been discarded by the thieves, realising that there was nothing of real value in it.

He reached the end of the road and turned to the left, where he saw a row of three small refuse bins. He opened each bin and frantically searched through the rubbish. Nothing! He slowly walked back towards the hotel feeling utterly sickened and deflated, all the while looking to his left and right up the narrow streets that fed off this main road.

It was then that he noticed something black protruding from a recess in a building up one of the alleyways. He excitedly ran over to the black bag. Yes, he was sure now it was a bag and it looked like his. As soon as he reached it, he realised it wasn't. It was much bigger. The zips had obviously been burst open and anything that had been in it was long gone.

He wasn't the only one who had had their bag stolen in Barcelona that day.

He walked forlornly back to the hotel. He could see Louise in the distance, standing in exactly the same place. She had taken his instructions to 'stay there' quite literally. She hadn't moved a muscle.

"Any luck?" she shouted.

"No." That was all David could think of saying. He felt sick. He felt violated. They stood in silence for what seemed like ages, but in fact it was only about thirty seconds. Then David seemed to come out of his trance.

"Let's go."

They grabbed a case each and went back into the hotel.

"We'll report the crime and ask someone in reception if we can we can have the use of a computer for a few minutes. I'll reprint the e-docs for the ship and the e-mail ticket for the flight home."

Louise was still very quiet, as for David, he was certainly thinking a bit clearer now.

Luckily, Maria was still in reception and David wasted no time in asking her advice, after he had told her their story. When she asked if he wanted to claim for the stolen goods through their insurance policy he immediately replied that they would, as he remembered he had one hundred and fifty pounds of English money (which Louise didn't know about) in his jeans pocket. There was also expensive perfume and after shave which Louise had bought in duty free, and they were all in the bag. She advised David to report the incident to the police, as a police report would certainly help with the insurance claim.

"Were there any witnesses David? That would help too."

He was sure that there must have been someone who had witnessed it, so he said yes and bolted from the reception desk, heading for the exit.

As he hurried towards the door, Maria shouted.

"You had better be quick, you only have one hour before your ship sails. Remember, you still have to get to the port from here."

'This is all I needed,' he thought to himself as he raced through the revolving doors,

'What a start to a holiday.'

Chapter 4
The Witness

David had noticed a man sitting on his balcony in an apartment straight across from the hotel and thought he might have seen everything, so he went to speak to him while Louise waited just outside the hotel. He crossed the street and shouted up to the man sitting on his fifth floor balcony.

"Do you speak English?" he asked.

"Yes. How can I help you?"

David was relieved to hear that the man could speak splendid English.

"We've just had our bag stolen and I was wondering if you saw it happening?"

"Yes I did, would you like to come up?" David then heard a buzzing sound, and the gate of the apartments' entrance slowly opened.

He ran up the stairs two at a time until he reached the fifth floor, and there in front of him was flat 503, door ajar and the man standing just inside the door. He was about five feet eight tall, late fifties; fat with a round red face, very short greying hair and he wore a pair of thin scrooge like glasses. They teetered on the end of his nose, which seemed too thin for his face. He wore black shoes, black trousers, a white shirt, which his belly pushed way over his straining belt, and a black cardigan.

"Come in," he said and introduced himself as Juan Marquez as he ushered David through to the balcony where there was a table, upon which sat four different cameras, all with different length lenses, and two chairs.

"I'm a professional photographer," he said to David as he saw him looking at the cameras.

He certainly had a beautiful view from this vantage point.

David introduced himself and thanked Juan for inviting him into his home and for speaking to him. He then waved down to Louise standing below. He asked Juan if he would give a statement to the police when they arrived, explaining that it was only necessary so that he (David) could get a police report to make it easier to make their insurance claim.

"No problem." said Juan.

"Did you see the young man come up and speak to me to take my attention?" asked David.

"Yes-- they call it mis-direction."

"And my wife" David started, but Juan interrupted asking,

"Is that your wife down there?" He pointed to Louise who was standing across the street.

"Yes that's her. Did you see another young man approaching her at the same time?"

"Yes."

"Did you see the man speaking to her?"

"No, he didn't speak to her."

David was a little surprised. "Did he not speak to her to distract her while he lifted the bag?"

"No. He approached your wife and she simply handed him the bag."

Chapter 5

David had met Louise thirty years previous, when he worked as a sales representative for a large confectionery company, and she worked as a model and promotions girl. His company were introducing a brand new product to the market and he had been selected to do the presentation and launch. He had planned the whole event, and to help with the distribution of samples and point of sales material to the invited audience, he had decided to hire two promotion girls.

This was the first time that he had seen Louise. She was about five feet six tall, had short blonde hair, obviously cut by a top hairdresser, lightly tanned skin, and he noticed she didn't wear any make-up. She wore a little black dress, which made her look slim, sexy and simply stunning. He was in love.

As for Louise she was attracted to David immediately. He was about the same height as her and although she preferred taller men, she was instantly hooked, when she saw his long eyelashes, jet-black hair, and that mischievous glint in his ice blue eyes.

David had asked her for a date that very night, and the following week he took her out to 'Michels', the top restaurant in her home town of Stirling. They had enjoyed a sumptuous meal and a wonderful evening, which was to be the first of many they would spend together. This was the start of their relationship.

After two years Louise moved into David's home, and they began to learn more about each other... their likes, dislikes, habits good and bad, their pasts and their problems. They went on holidays to Spain, Italy, France, Germany, Austria, and America, as well as many city breaks to cities throughout Britain. They had a great time. They eventually decided to get married eight years later, when Louise had intimated that she wanted to start a family.

They were married in St Aloysius Church, Chapelhall, a small village in Lanarkshire, in the West of Scotland, where David was born.

That was twenty years ago and during that period they had plenty of ups and downs, numerous arguments, and many bouts of long silences. They had encountered money problems, (more than once), housing problems, trust problems, drinking problems, work problems and worst of all baby problems. Louise had lost a baby and was then told she couldn't have any more, and she had suffered severe bouts of depression for years. They had come through all that together.

They knew each other inside out, or did they?

Chapter 6

David slowly walked back down the stairs from Juan Marquez's apartment. He couldn't take in what he had told him. He walked through the gate, crossed the road, and through the revolving doors back into the hotel. He was in a daze. He couldn't believe that he now doubted Louise.... his wife, his soulmate. Someone whom he had known for thirty years through thick and thin, for good or for bad, in sickness and in health. Even more so was the reason why he doubted her.

He had spoken to a complete stranger for no more than five minutes, and he believed him more than he believed her.

He was now standing in the hotel lobby and he immediately noticed Louise sitting on one of the many bright orange sofas that half filled the reception area. She was talking to a middle-aged man who was wearing a beautiful black silk suit. It appeared to David that she somehow knew this man. David shook his head and thought to himself that paranoia was definitely setting in. How could she possibly know this man?

Maria snapped him out of his trance when she called his name, "Mr Telfer did you find your witness?" she enquired.

David turned round and hesitantly replied "yes."

"Are you alright?" she asked, noticing that he looked rather anxious.

"Yes I'm ok, but I'm not too sure about my witness."

"What's his name?"

"Juan Marquez. He lives in apartment 503, just across the road. But I'm not too happy with what he has just told me."

"Why? What did he say?"

"He told me that Louise just handed our bag to that guy... he didn't steal it! That just can't be true."

"Do not listen to a word he says," said Maria, "he is a petty thief himself. He has been involved in stealing all of his life. We actually have reason to believe that he is the lookout for certain gangs of thieves and pickpockets who work this area. We think he tips them off when our guests are leaving the hotel. In fact that's what may have happened with you and your wife. He would say anything to help his gang of thieves! I will ask the police to have a word with him."

David was overwhelmed with a terrible sense of guilt! He had believed that bastard.

He then felt a sea of relief envelop his whole body and he started to laugh out loud, just through sheer joy. Everyone turned round and looked at him in surprise, but he didn't care. He simply looked over to Louise, smiled and waved.

He no longer doubted her.

Chapter 7

David walked back outside through the revolving doors. He needed some fresh air. His head was throbbing, and all kinds of thoughts flashed through his mind regarding the morning's goings on. He just stood there, in the middle of the pavement. He didn't know what to do next. After a few minutes he regained his composure, went back into reception, and asked Maria if she would call the police.

"They are here already. I hope you don't mind, but I contacted the police while you were looking for your witness. I thought it would save you some time. Let me introduce you."

"Not at all, thanks for your help once again. What would I do without you? Every time I'm in Barcelona I need you to sort out some problem for me."

He followed her over to where Louise and the gentleman in the black suit were sitting. The man stood up and Maria introduced him as Senor Gilberto Ramirez, Assistant Chief of the Mossos d'Esquadra (one of the three different police forces which look after the people and visitors of Barcelona).

He was about six feet tall, late fifties, immaculately dressed in his suit, crisp white shirt and black shoes that were polished to a gleaming finish. He had black hair and a black moustache both of which were clearly dyed. He had a swarthy complexion, and had obviously had acne problems as a youngster.

"Thank you for coming so quickly" David said to Senor Ramirez as he shook his hand.

"Not a problem, I was actually just passing the hotel when the call came in," said Senor Ramirez, "I'm sorry you had to call the police in the first place. I have spoken to your wife already, so if you would like to take a seat, you can tell me your version of what happened and I will write a report for you. I will have it ready for you when you return from your cruise. I believe you are staying here for two nights after your cruise?"

"Yes we are" said David, and he proceeded to tell his story of the bag theft, which seemed to have taken place so long ago now. Senor Ramirez took notes as David spoke. The interview only lasted five minutes and then all three stood up. Senor Ramirez wished them a happy holiday, and then said his goodbyes.

David asked Maria if he could use the computer to reprint the e-docs for boarding the ship, and the tickets for the flight home.

"Certainly" said Maria, "but you don't need to reprint your booking for this hotel, in fact I've just upgraded your room for your return. There is also a taxi waiting for you outside, compliments of the hotel. You only have half an hour until the ship sails. I hope you make it in time."

David then printed everything he needed, thanked her for all her help and said he would see her when he returned. He turned to Louise and gave her a peck on the cheek.

"Let's forget this ever happened and just enjoy our holiday. Surely things can only get better from here on in."

He took Louise by the hand and they both rushed out of the hotel.

Chapter 8

Outside the taxi was waiting just as Maria had promised. David ushered Louise towards the car, and pulled the two cases forward to the kerb side. The taxi driver opened the door for Louise, and she slid into the back seat. David paused just before entering the car. He rested his right arm on top of the open door and looked up to see if Juan Marquez was looking, and sure enough, there he was, sitting on his balcony, on the fifth floor, watching everything that was going on. David just shook his head and wondered how he could have possibly believed that lying bastard, but he couldn't help but still have doubts about what Marquez had said. He couldn't see what he had to gain by telling lies.

"Hurry up. Get in. We're going to miss the ship." Louise's words shook David from his train of thought and he slid into the taxi beside her. It pleased him to see that she certainly seemed to be feeling much better now. She smiled, grabbed his arm and cosied up to him.

"The Port please" he told the driver and kissed Louise on the forehead.

As the taxi slowly moved off, he decided to put Juan Marquez to the back of his mind...but something else was nagging him.

He didn't believe Senor Ramirez when he said he was 'just passing the hotel'. Any high ranking police officer that David knew would never have attended a call-in for such an incident, and so, it raised the question:

With all the thefts, burglaries, rapes and murders taking place everyday in Barcelona, why on earth had the Assistant Chief of Police come out personally and taken their statements, regarding the theft of one small insignificant bag?

Chapter 9

They were finally on their way to the Moll D'ossat terminal B, where their ship 'The American Gem' was berthed. They felt really excited as they looked out at some of the wonderful architecture that could be seen in Barcelona, and they decided they would forget about the bag incident which was all in the past now, and it had been dealt with anyway.

'For now at least' David thought to himself, as he anxiously looked at his watch.

He was now worried about Louise

She had lost her baby at birth, twelve years previous, and for six years afterwards she wasn't able to go back to work. She withdrew from normal life, and for two years after her loss she never left the house. She felt safe there.

David's employers had been very helpful and allowed him six months compassionate leave to help Louise through this difficult time. After the six months, David had to return to work, but only did so after consultation with her doctor and psychiatrist both of who thought that it might actually help her, by giving her some space. They had both noted that Louise's state of mind had certainly improved, but still had to be closely monitored. David returned to work which certainly helped him get some kind of normality back into his life, but it was very difficult when he returned home in the evening to find Louise sitting in the dark withdrawn into her own little world.

However after several months there was certainly some improvement in her condition, but he knew it only took the most trivial incident, or the slightest stress to send her into a deep depression. Like the time when she broke a plate while washing the dishes. David had come home that night to find the house ransacked, and Louise had barricaded herself in her room by pushing a wardrobe against the door.

David didn't see her for a week. She only came out of her room when he had gone to work, have something to eat, do what she had to do, and get back into her room before he came home. He wasn't sure how to handle that situation, but decided he would 'go with the flow', and sure enough at the end of the week she came out of the room and carried on as if nothing had happened. He had to deal with many such incidents but he loved her so much that he just dealt with everything that was thrown his way. After lots of patience he finally managed to get her to go out of the house. This helped her immensely and her condition showed great signs of improvement, so much so that her doctor decided to cut down her medication.

The fact that she was now going out brought a different set of problems for David. She was still on medication but she had started drinking, and now when some incident sent her into depression, she handled it differently now. She would just disappear for days on end.

Once, she disappeared for a whole month, when something had pushed her over the edge, (David never found out what), and she decided to go to London to meet up with her best friend from her modelling days, Danielle. She had a spare room and she let Louise stay, as she knew she had problems, and at least she could keep an eye on her. Danielle was also clever enough to persuade Louise to give her David's phone number so that she could let him know she was safe. This was after three weeks. David waited patiently and sure enough she returned home the following week.

This escapade actually signalled the start of her real recovery, as Danielle had offered to help Louise by giving her a part-time job. She owned a modelling agency, 'Mature Models', and had offices in both London and Glasgow. She didn't just offer Louise a job through pity, she knew that she had been a great model in her younger days, she knew the business, and she had definitely retained her good looks.

Louise started work in the Glasgow office, part-time at first, but it wasn't long before she said that Danielle wanted her to become full-time and go with her for her first overseas assignment to Barcelona. After that trip, she said that Danielle had asked her to take on more European work, as she was in such big demand due to her good looks and hard work ethic.

So six years after she lost her baby, Louise was finally well on the road to recovery due to the care, attention and correct medication given by her doctor and psychiatrist, but as they put it, mainly due to David's patience and love. The fact that Danielle had given Louise a job had also been a major factor in the healing process as it had given her back her independence, self-esteem, and self-confidence. So much so, that in the following six years she had travelled to Dublin, London, Paris, Munich, Venice, Rome and Madrid, all on modelling assignments.

This was their first holiday together for twelve years, as a celebration of her complete recovery, but as they sat in the back of that taxi, David couldn't help having doubts about Louise. She had put him through hell over the years, and had always expected him to be there for her, when she came out of her "depression" or "tantrum", or whatever you wanted to call it. He sometimes thought that she wasn't depressed, but in fact was just playing on his good nature and just stringing him along. Making him do the shopping, the housework, and everything else that needed to be done, while she sat in the house and did zilch, because she was in a depression.

He found it hard to actually believe that she was completely recovered. He just hoped that the trauma of the bag theft didn't trigger any of her old thoughts and feelings, and send her spiralling into a deep depression, because at the end of the day, he still loved her.

Chapter 10
Juan Marquez

Juan Marquez had been abandoned by his parents at birth, but that still didn't give him an excuse for the kind of life that he led. He was put into care, and was brought up by the nuns of the La Sagrada Familia, (the same name as Gaudi's famous cathedral) who lived in a convent on the outskirts of Barcelona. They had tried their best to control him, but it was evident from a very early age that Juan was a total tearaway.

He had started stealing when he was seven years of age, when he and his friends would go into his local sweet shop en masse, and while his friends distracted the shop-keeper, he would put the sweets into his pocket or bag. He was their leader and they all looked up to him.

At thirteen years of age he ran away from the convent, along with another kid the same age, Carlos Angel Martinez and decided to ply his trade in the centre of Barcelona. They managed to 'get in' with a group of older boys all aged about eighteen who squatted in an apartment block located in one of the rundown areas of the city, a place never frequented by tourists. Although the older boys bullied them at first, they soon realised that these young boys had talent and Juan and Carlos soon became respected members of their fraternity (if that word 'respected' can be used in these circumstances).

They used to practice their pick pocketing skills on each other in the squat, and the older boys taught them new techniques. They then took the metro into Barcelona city centre and started their work. Indeed they started as soon as they hit the metro, as it was always busy, with people squeezing themselves onto the trains......ideal conditions for professional pickpockets.

However they preferred places like La Boqueria--St Joseph's market in Las Ramblas, Barcelona Cathedral, or the Placa Catalunya at the top of Las Ramblas, because these areas were packed with tourists who were very naïve and easy to pick out.

Juan and Carlos were a great pairing and it wasn't too long before they were bringing in plenty of money for the group. That was the way it worked. Everybody put all the money that they had stolen into the kitty, and the leader, Diego Morales at that time, shared it out equally (so he claimed) among everyone. That had seemed fair when they had joined the group, but now as eighteen year olds who were bringing in the most money by far, Juan and Carlos were none too happy with that process, and decided to leave the commune and set up their own.

Diego didn't like the sound of this proposal and he did what any gang leader would have done.

He summoned them to a meeting.

Diego ruled by fear, and there was no way he was going to let his two best earners walk out on him to set up on their own.

The meeting consisted of a terrible beating for both Juan and Carlos, which must have lasted a full five minutes. Diego had his three top henchmen on tow, and he had instructed them to start on Juan as soon as he had entered the room, using their baseball bats as weapons. This they had done with great pleasure, and after about a minute, just as they had expected, Carlos jumped in to help Juan.

They nearly killed them both.

Diego ordered an end to the horrific onslaught, and then casually walked over and kicked both Juan and Carlos as they lay in agony.

"You will not leave my gang until I tell you. I will decide who stays and who leaves. You try to leave and the two of you are fucking dead men!!!"

He spat on them and walked away laughing.

It was two weeks before Juan and Carlos were fit enough to work the streets again for Diego. During that time they gave a lot of thought to the predicament they found themselves in. They came to the conclusion that it would not have been beneficial to their state of health to leave the commune at this point in time.

They had another plan.

One month later Diego Morales and his three henchmen were found dead in the squat. They each had been killed by one bullet to the head, executioner style. No one said a word. Everyone knew who had shot them.

Juan and Carlos had become the leaders of the pack.

Chapter 11

They could see their ship through the side windows of their taxi, as it sped around the bend and down the hill which lead to terminal B. They heard three loud blasts of the ship's horn and David shouted out—"Oh no, we're too late!" as he glanced at his watch.

"Seven minutes to four" he said, "the ship's leaving early. It's not supposed to leave until four."

Just then Louise screamed, "Look! Look over at the terminal entrance!"

They were both overjoyed because they could clearly see a steward wearing a high viz jacket holding up a board with their names on it...'Mr and Mrs David Telfer.'

It was obvious that he was waiting for them and hopefully he would escort them onto the ship without any hold-ups. They got out of the taxi and the driver took their cases out of the boot.

"Thank you for getting us here in time. I think you could give Fernando Alonso a run for his money" said David as he handed him thirty euros for the fare.

The driver laughed and said, "gratias senor", but it was clear that he had no idea what David had said. He grabbed the money, hurriedly jumped into his cab and sped off.

Alan, the steward, took the case from Louise and said, "This way please, madam". He sounded French.

Five minutes to four.

David and Louise followed him into the terminal building and over to a very, very, very long check-in counter, and there in the distance, at the opposite end stood one young girl, patiently waiting to check them in. When they reached her, David nervously looked at his watch.

Four minutes to four.

She only asked them two questions, their names and their method of payment on board ship.

Three minutes to four.

She then gave them each their personal card, which would serve as the key of their room as well as a credit card for all purchases made on the ship

"Please hurry," said Alan "I'm afraid you won't have any time for duty free".

Two minutes to four.

"Don't worry about that," said David as he and Louise scurried up the stairs, which lead to the boarding deck—deck 7. The wheels of David's case weren't even touching the ground.

They still weren't sure if they were going to be able to board.

However all their fears disappeared as they reached the last stair, as there before them was the walkway reaching across to the ship, and onboard a group of the ship's crew all clapping and cheering, throwing streamers, and holding red, white and blue balloon clusters.

One minute to four.

Another crew member held a tray with two glasses of champagne on it, which he offered to Louise and David. They gratefully accepted. Security then asked them for their key cards which he passed through the card checker. He gave them back their cards and invited them to go through the doors which opened onto the atrium.

Four o'clock and they heard the ship's horn give one final blast. They opened the doors and were greeted by a wall of people, some staff but mostly guests.

Some were just walking around looking at the surroundings in amazement, some were standing at the bar asking for drinks, and some were just sitting in the large comfy purple settees that adorned the atrium. The sound of laughter and chat filled the air.

In the background they could just hear the sound of a piano playing, and as the crowds split in front of them, they could see 'Pierre' seated at his huge gleaming black piano, playing Scott Joplin's theme from 'The Sting'. It sounded wonderful.

"Very appropriate piece of music," David said to Louise.

"What do you mean"?

"I mean, I've just remembered that the taxi was compliments of the hotel and I've just given the driver another thirty euros....... and the bastard took it!"

Louise and David just looked at each other and both burst into fits of laughter.

Chapter 12

Carlos Angel Martinez

Carlos and Juan had found themselves at the head of a pickpocket gang at the age of eighteen. Carlos was very ambitious, clever and shrewd and had big plans to clean up the dirty money they were making, by using it in legitimate business. Juan was holding him back and had been for several years now, but he had carried him along with him. Juan had descended into a world of drugs because he had easy access to them, and he now had the money to buy ever-increasing amounts of cocaine.

Carlos had decided to just carry on re-organising the business and left Juan to his own devices hoping that some day he would see the light. He would help him all he could, he thought, but Juan would have to buck his ideas up soon or he would have to get rid of him. In the meantime he would set about the re-structuring by himself, and his first decision was to give all of his pickpockets a wage that they would receive every week without fail. They all agreed.

He started a 'credit card department' as he called it, because he realised more and more tourists were using cards. This meant that he actually employed criminals, who as experts on credit cards, knew exactly how to extract the money from these poor people's accounts.

His pickpockets would steal them, give them to him, and he would give them to his 'credit card department' who immediately started emptying the accounts before they were cancelled.

He also employed eight and nine year olds who he positioned at the cash dispensers throughout the city. He discreetly placed tiny mirrors above the keyboards of the dispensers and while the unsuspecting victim keyed in their pin number, the small villains would just look up, smile and memorise the number which they could see in the mirror because of their small stature. (These small thieves had to be below a certain height before he would employ them)

They would then give the signal to their pickpocket accomplice nearby and they would steal the bank card.

After a few years, Carlos had amassed thirty four million pesetas (more than two hundred thousand euros) and he had decided to move onto the next level of his strategy.

He employed a lawyer and instructed him to start buying property in Barcelona, which he had already targeted. This was the first part of his plan to cleanse his dirty money.

During these few years Juan's condition, as regards to his drug problem, had deteriorated badly and his dependency to drugs had reached an all time high.

The time had come.

Juan had become a drawback and a constant drain on Carlos' resources.

He could not allow this, and had made up his mind. He had to go! There was no place for a weakling like Juan in his empire. For this indeed was the start of an empire.

He had no intention of killing him, so he just instructed two of his henchmen to take him to Barcelona cathedral and leave him at the entrance to the priests' quarters, in the hope that they would be able to help him.

Even in his drug-fuelled stupor, Juan realised what was happening to him, and he called out to the two men as they walked away from him,

"You tell that bastard Carlos I'll get him back one day, he owes me!"

Chapter 13

Now at the age of fifty-nine, Carlos was a multi millionaire with over thirty hotels in Barcelona. He owned four beautiful homes, five if you counted the one his wife didn't know about, and was a much respected member of the community who was about to run for Mayor of Barcelona.

He was married to Teresa, who at sixty-nine years of age, was ten years his senior. She had been a beautiful woman in her day.

She had been a model in her younger days, and he had met her while she was working on a photo shoot in front of Gaudi's famous building "La Padrera" in Passeig de Gracia.

He had also been working there, as a pickpocket, because that was one of the busiest tourist attractions in Barcelona. He had pursued her from that first sight, and had eventually won her over with his good looks and sweet talk. He had said to his friend that very day, "I will marry her one day." Three years later he did.

They had one son, Miguel, aged twenty-nine who lived in Madrid with his wife and two children. He worked as an accountant. Carlos's marriage seemed to be a marriage made in heaven, and it had to be seen that way, in order for him to achieve his goals. He was a celebrity in Barcelona because of his charity work, and he was well known for his generous donations to many charities. Everything in his life now had to be seen to be squeaky clean, but if some of his present social activities were to be discovered, he could forget about becoming mayor. But he also couldn't help thinking that something or someone from his past might come back to haunt him and ruin his plans.

He had not seen Juan from that day he had abandoned him all those years ago, and now he couldn't get him out of his mind. As for Juan, he thought about Carlos everyday of his life, and indeed had seen him many times since he moved into his apartment 503, straight across from one of his hotels, the Hotel Sants.

Juan was still waiting for his chance.

Chapter 14

The ship was a colossus, a marvel of modern technology and a credit to man's shipbuilding skills and creative talents. The American Gem weighed 200,000 tons and stood nineteen decks high, 1440 feet long, the length of four soccer pitches, and had a passenger capacity of five thousand two hundred and thirty six. In total, it had two thousand six hundred staterooms, inside, outside, or balcony cabins and sixty penthouse, de luxe or villa suites. These sixty suites could be found on decks sixteen and seventeen, and their occupants had access to their own private secluded swimming pool with three hot tubs, gym and sauna, which could be found in a beautiful shared courtyard. They all came with butler service and could only be accessed by private elevator.

This is where the 'elite" stayed on this ship.

Louise had wanted to book one of these suites, but it just wasn't possible on their income. Her father was a very wealthy man and in her younger days she was used to getting what she wanted. Money was no object to her father, however things had changed dramatically since then, and her father didn't speak to David as he thought he wasn't good enough or rich enough for his daughter.

They were staying in inside stateroom 9067, one of the most affordable living spaces, but nevertheless very nice and compact. It had a wonderful king size bed, en suite toilet and bathroom with shower, two seater sofa, coffee table, twenty six inch flat screen television, and a beautiful mahogany mirrored dressing table with chair and matching wardrobe. Part of that lovely unit was a refrigerator fully stocked with miniatures of wine, spirits, water and soft drinks. Built into the wardrobe was their personal safe with four-figure combination. David always used the four figures of his and Louise's age, this time being 5248. They were extremely happy with their room and decided, after a small aperitif and a change of clothes that they would explore the rest of the ship.

While Louise went into the bathroom and changed into her black bikini, sarong and comfortable sandals, David put on his swimming shorts, tee shirt and flip-flops and had a vodka and diet coke from the fridge while he waited. She was ready quicker than usual so David just took his drink with him, and they both caught the glass elevator up to the fifteenth floor where the outdoor pool and bar were situated.

They collected two towels from the 'complimentary towel station', and managed to find two sun beds just next to the pool but still quite close to the bar, so that they didn't need to walk too far for their drinks. They needn't have worried, as there were plenty of waiters, dressed in brightly coloured Hawaiian shirts and khaki shorts working around the pool area.

"Drinks?" they would ask as they passed by, while spinning their shiny circular aluminium tray on their index finger. After finishing his vodka David finally took one of them up on his offer.

"Louise would you like a drink?"

"Yes."

"What would you like?"

"Surprise me!"

"Ok. Two pina coladas please waiter". David then asked him his name and where he came from.

"Its Rupino sir, I come from Manila, in the Philippines."

"The land of Manny Pacquaio! What a boxer!" David quipped.

"Yes sir" he said excitedly, "Do you know that when one of his fights is on TV, everyone stops whatever they are doing and watches his fight. He is a living legend. When he finishes his boxing career, we want him to become president of our country."

"Who are 'we' Rupino?"

"The people of the Philippines sir," and noticing that Louise was beginning to look slightly agitated he added, "do you want small or large pina coladas sir, and can I have your card please?"

"Make it two large, Rupino please", Louise suddenly interjected, and rose up from her sun bed.

"My feet are not comfortable in these shoes," she said as she stood up and smoothed out her sarong. "I'm going down to change them, I'll be back in five minutes," and she walked away.

While she was gone, Rupino returned with the drinks. He placed them down on the table, gave David his card back and asked him to sign one of the two receipts that he passed down to him in his waiter's leather bill presenter. David signed and returned it and watched Rupino turn and walk away alongside the swimming pool, calling out "Drinks anyone?" He seemed a nice guy.

After an hour, Louise still hadn't returned and David started to get worried, as he knew she had a terrible sense of direction and was probably wandering about the ship somewhere, not having a clue where she was. He decided to go look for her, so he finished his drink, walked to the nearest elevator and pushed the downward arrow. Just as he did so, the elevator bell rang and the doors opened and there she was, still in her bikini and sarong, but she had indeed changed her shoes.

She was wearing black stiletto high heels.

He was dumbstruck.

In all of their holidays together throughout the years, he had never ever seen her dressed like this.

Had his fears come true?

Had she snapped? Was this her alter ego, and was this her way of dealing with her trauma of the bag theft, trivial though it seemed to David now?

This was Louise the model, not Louise the person.

As she walked out of the lift and passed him she asked,

"Did you get me my pina colada?"

"Yes" was all David could say in his state of surprise, as he turned and followed her like her pet dog. But he couldn't help noticing that the number of the previous floor, from where the lift had come... number 17.

'How the hell could Louise have come from deck seventeen, the living quarters of the 'elite', when you need a special pass key to reach that floor? What is going on here?' he thought to himself. 'There must be a simple explanation.'

But that thought went right out of his mind as he watched her walk over to the sun beds and he mumbled to himself.

"My god she is gorgeous!"

Chapter 15

Juan Marquez was well known to the police and had been for many years. They knew that he never had a proper job, but he always seemed to have money from his criminal activities, although they couldn't prove that, because he had never been caught and prosecuted.

He had no criminal record.

He now stayed in apartment 503, across the street from the Hotel Sants, and had been there for the last fifteen years. There were two reasons for this.

The first was that he had been asked to move into the apartment by one of the local pickpocket / bag snatcher gangs who actually owned the flat and they had a job for him. They had known Juan as a thief for years, and the fact that he didn't have a police record was a bonus as it wouldn't raise any suspicions with the other residents in the block, as they had a say in who could live there. So Juan moved in without any problems.

The job he was given was that of a lookout. He would tip them off when guests were leaving the hotel to catch taxis to the port or airport, or indeed to anywhere in Barcelona.

He was an experienced bag snatcher so he could tell at a glance if anyone was ripe and ready for the picking, and this allowed the gang to work elsewhere, if he informed them that it wasn't worth visiting the Sants area. He saved them a lot of time and found them many, many victims, as this was a large and popular hotel, very close to the railway station.

They paid him for this information.

The second reason was that this hotel belonged to Carlos Angel Martinez, and he had become obsessed by getting his own back on his former 'friend', who had abandoned him all those years ago. He watched Carlos when he visited the Hotel Sants, which he used to do quite regularly, as he was a boss who made sure his hotels were being run properly.

He would turn up unannounced and carry out a hotel inspection. This kept all his staff on their toes. He would sometimes stay for a few nights and sample the hotel restaurant food and service.

Juan watched him come and go and Carlos didn't even notice him. He didn't know where Juan stayed, and although most of his staff knew where Juan lived, they never even thought of telling Mr.Martinez, because they didn't know of any connection between them.

Juan used to take photographs of him as he moved in and out of the hotel, or walked along the street to the Café Magic at the end of the road. Juan was definitely obsessed with Carlos Angel Martinez and he hoped that one day he would photograph him meeting some underground criminal, or in some compromising position, and he could then fuck up his election campaign by selling the snaps to the media. Either that or he could blackmail him and extort some of the money from Martinez that Juan felt was rightfully his, from all those years ago.

This was actually another way in which he made money, without moving from his flat.

He ran a small blackmailing scam along with an accomplice from within the hotel...an insider!

Chapter 16

Juan was a brilliant photographer, although not a professional one, which he told everyone when asked what he did for a living. He certainly made a living from taking pictures and developing them in his own dark room, situated in the small back room of his apartment. But the photographs that he took were not your normal photos of happy times, birthdays, parties, weddings or holidays; he took snaps of people without their permission. This was all part of his scam, which he had used for the last twelve years.

It was all so simple.

He had a deal with one of the hotel receptionists, Alfonso, who obviously had access to all the names, addresses, and telephone numbers of all the hotel guests. After thirty-five years in the hotel game, he also had a nose for working out which couples were actually married to each other, and which ones were having an illicit affair, or a one-night stand with someone who was not 'their wife or husband'.

He was brilliant at it.

He enjoyed the challenge of the game, and the buzz he got from guessing correctly.

He also enjoyed the money he received from Juan if he was right. All he had to do was to follow them out of the hotel and discreetly point them out to Juan who would be waiting on his balcony, and he would do the rest.

Juan would then take photographs of them hopefully holding hands, kissing, or acting all 'lovey dovey' as they walked down the street. If he was lucky they would be staying in a room at the side of the building, which faced his apartment. Alfonso would contact him with the room number, and he would know exactly which room they were in. He had lived across the road from the hotel for fifteen years and he knew exactly which room was which.

Juan would then sit with his camera at the ready, with various telescopic and infrared lenses at hand and stakeout that room, waiting for the couple returning to the room for the night.

Amazingly he found that most couples who are more than a few floors up, always leave their curtains open at night, especially in the hot weather, and this enabled him to take some very intimate pictures of the said couples in different stages of undress, and in some very compromising positions.

He would then simply develop the photos and send them off to the address given to him by Alfonso. It was usually the address of the man, but Juan didn't care either way, he would send it to the woman if Alfonso felt that she was the 'married' one.

He would send them to various parts of the world, as well as locally. It always surprised him how far people would travel for a few nights of illicit sex. He would also enclose a letter with the photos, stating that if he or she wanted the remaining snaps destroyed, then all they had to do was to return a cheque for one thousand euros made out to a phoney business for which he had set up an account, and return it to the P.O. Box address he had given them. He also promised that he would never contact them again after they had returned the cheque. Then he would just wait.

If Alfonso had got it correct, then Juan would receive a cheque in the post. If not then that was it finished, as Alfonso had got it wrong and the couple were not in the least concerned, although maybe a little puzzled. It never ceased to amaze Juan how many times Alfonso got it right and they received cheques.

Sometimes a letter would accompany a cheque for maybe only six or seven hundred euros, stating that this was all they could afford. Juan didn't mind, it was better than nothing.

No one ever tried to find out who was doing this to them, they were too frightened their 'affair' would be brought out into the open, so they just paid the money and kept their mouths shut.

He had made quite a lot of money over the years and now he was only hoping that he could catch someone famous in one of his snapshots, and he could ask for even more money.

Of course there were plenty of quiet times, and Juan would just take random pictures of couples in the hotel rooms facing him. He would wait until it was dark and then go out onto his balcony and into his secret hideout and start clicking away, in the hope of hitting the jackpot.

This is exactly what he had done on Saturday night, the 5th of September.

Chapter 17

On that Saturday night he had been sitting on his balcony having a few glasses of wine, and keeping his eyes open for any action. This was his usual Saturday night, although it was now two o'clock in the morning and he would have expected to have seen some before this.

He noticed the lights being switched on in room 705 straight across from him, but two floors higher, and he immediately went into his secret camera position in the corner of his balcony.

Juan's balcony was covered with all sorts of flowers and plants which he really enjoyed nurturing and cultivating, however he had another reason for having so many on his balcony.

He had grown some of the shrubs and climbing ivy in such a way that he created a secret hiding place from which he could take his photographs and not be seen. When he was in there, it was impossible to see him or his camera lens. It was a brilliant piece of camouflage.

The couple were standing just at the other side of the sliding glass door, which led onto the balcony, each holding what looked like a glass of wine. He couldn't make out their faces as they were too far away and the lights were now dimmed, but his lens would soon sort that out for him.

They then started kissing and the woman started to undress slowly and provocatively. Juan could only see her from the waist up, so he didn't know if she was completely undressed, but he knew for sure that she was naked on top, as he started to take his pictures of her beautiful rounded breasts and slim lithe torso. The man had now managed to get his shirt off, just before she pushed him back against the wall and started to kiss him passionately.

Juan was snapping like hell.

And then the curtains closed.

But he had taken plenty of pictures and he was sure that when he developed, lightened and enlarged them, he would be able to make out their faces without any problems

He would wait until Monday or Tuesday, depending on when Alfonso was working, to contact him to find out the names of the couple that had stayed in room 705, and to ask him if he thought they were worth blackmailing. He wouldn't develop the pictures until then.

He would just have to wait and see if he had struck it lucky!

Chapter 18
The Cop

Gilberto Ramirez, the Assistant Head of police, sat in his office mulling over the statements he had taken from David and Louise Telfer, as he looked out of the window at the bright Barcelona sun. It was a lovely Monday morning, although just like the Boomtown Rats' song, 'he didn't like Mondays.' He also didn't like the fact that he had to write out a report for a stupid bag theft which had taken place outside the Hotel Sants the previous day, but he had no choice. Gilberto was a long time associate and friend of one Carlos Angel Martinez, the owner of the hotel.

Their paths had first crossed when he was about twenty-two years of age and he had just joined the Mossos d'Esquadra. He was young and ambitious, and he didn't want to see his home city of Barcelona become a haven for all sorts of thieves, conmen and reprobates.

He didn't want his hometown to gain the reputation of "crime capital of Europe".

He thought he could make a difference.

At first he and his partner would go out on the beat to scour for pickpockets around the tourist haunts like Barcelona Cathedral or the Magic Fountain in Plaza Espagna. These places were always packed with tourists.......tourists meant pickpockets.

Usually their presence would be enough to deter the thieves, but there were always some who just ignored them and continued their thieving ways, directly in front of them.

Gilberto and his partner used to arrest these characters on the spot and take them to the station, but they would only be in a cell for maybe two hours and then they would be let back out onto the streets.

This disgusted and annoyed Gilberto.

While carrying out these duties he realised that he was dealing with another problem—drugs. When he looked into the eyes of some of these thieves he could see that they were 'on something', and realised that they were stealing to feed their habit.

But he knew that their problem was of their own doing, and that he was only trying to do his own job and trying to clean up the streets of Barcelona.

Gilberto and his partner were very successful and made many arrests, but soon discovered that for every arrest, they had to fill in many forms and file a report.

They were soon overwhelmed with paperwork.

This was not the way that Gilberto had foreseen the work of a policeman. He was fighting a losing battle, and crime figures were on the rise.

Two years on the force and he hadn't made one iota of a difference. He was becoming disillusioned.

It was about this time that he first met Carlos, when he had just arrested one of Carlos' boys. Carlos had appeared just as he was taking the boy to the police station to be charged, walking him along the street with his hands handcuffed behind his back. Gilberto was on his own as his partner had slipped away for a cigarette. Carlos approached him and said that he was the boy's guardian, and that he was very sorry for any trouble that he had caused, before adding,

"Is there any way we can handle this without it going any further? I mean just think about all that paperwork!"

"I like paperwork" Gilberto answered, which he knew was a total lie!

Gilberto had been given a telling off from one of his superiors that very morning and was in a foul mood, and the last thing he wanted to do was to have to start writing out a report that he would have to hand to that pompous bastard.

"What do you suggest?"

"This", said Carlos as he handed him a five thousand-peseta note (approx thirty euros).

He hesitated for a second, put the money in his pocket and then opened the handcuffs and let the boy run away. Carlos introduced himself properly and said that if Gilberto looked after his boys, then there would be a lot more of the same, if he was interested. That was it! He had taken the money, there was no going back.

Now, all these years later Gilberto knew that he would never have reached the position he was now in, if it had not been for Carlos Angel Martinez. As Carlos had become wealthier and more powerful, he had gained access to the inner circles of some very high-powered individuals, like top policemen and politicians. He had used his influence to push Gilberto up the career ladder until he was Assistant Head of police, for this not only helped Gilberto, it helped him, to have such a high ranking officer "on his side".

That is why Gilberto was in his office that sunny Monday morning writing that report, because he had been in the pocket of Carlos for thirty-seven years, and if Carlos had instructed him to write it personally, as he had, then he had no choice.

Chapter 19

It was Monday morning on board ship, and David and Louise were having breakfast in the Café Carousel, the ship's only self-service restaurant. After having a good look around all of the food on offer, David had decided on a cheese and ham omelette, three slice of bacon and two slice of toast. The omelette looked beautiful, and he had watched the chef cook it as he waited for his toast. Everything was freshly made. He then grabbed a glass of fresh orange juice, freshly squeezed of course, and went to look for a table.

Louise had also decided on a cheese omelette, one slice of toast, and instead of orange juice, a cup of tea, milk and no sugar. Both of them spotted a table over by the port side window and immediately made their way towards it as quick as they could, as the café was really busy and someone might have taken it at any moment.

They made it, and both let out a satisfying sigh.....'ahhhhhh'", as they both sat down at the same time.

"Look at that view!" said David, "isn't that just beautiful?"

"Just lovely", replied Louise as she started eating her breakfast.

David hadn't mentioned the "high heels" incident from the day before, when they were out the previous night, but he thought he would broach the subject over breakfast this morning, especially as she was wearing the shoes that just yesterday, she had said were uncomfortable.

"Aren't those the shoes that you had on yesterday?"

"Yes. Why?"

"Well, yesterday you said that they were uncomfortable and you went and changed them, and come to think of it, what were the high heels all about?"

"Why? Didn't you like them?"

"I don't think they were appropriate for wearing around the pool with your bikini!"

"Look" said Louise, "they were the only shoes I could get. I couldn't find the key of the other case, which contained all of my other shoes. That's all there was to it. Okay?"

"Okay! One more question. How come, when I met you coming out of the lift one hour later, the elevator came down from the seventeenth deck, why was that?"

Louise looked a little flustered, but within two seconds, she fired back, "What is this, the Spanish Inquisition? I was lost, and when I got into that elevator, one of the waiters was already in it, taking room service to someone in one of the suites on deck seventeen. He inadvertently swiped his pass card in the elevator, and it took us to deck seventeen. When he realised his mistake, he brought me back down to deck fifteen. Happy?"

"Okay, lighten up! Did you get out of the elevator? Were you not able to see any of the suites or the private pool? I would love to see up there!"

"No. I asked the waiter, but he said he would lose his job if he had allowed that."

David knew that he had angered Louise so he was just trying to ease the tension, but he also knew that something wasn't right with Louise.

He knew her too well.

Chapter 20

That Monday morning Juan Marquez, at exactly the same time, was calling Alfonso on his mobile phone.

"Good morning Alfonso, I need to know who was in room 705 on Saturday night. Can you help me please?"

"I'll try and find out for you sir, and I will call you right back."

Juan knew, by his tone, that someone had interrupted Alfonso and that he would call him back as soon as he got rid of his intruder. He poured himself a fresh cup of coffee, and went to sit out on his balcony in the warmth of the Barcelona sunshine, to wait for his return call. Two minutes later his phone buzzed.

"There was no one in room 705 on Saturday night, Juan. Are you sure you've got the correct number?"

"Of course I'm sure. I know all of the room numbers off by heart! Look I will double check and phone you back."

Juan looked across at the hotel, and in his mind he counted out all of the room numbers.

He was positive. It was room 705, no doubt. He dialled Alfonso's number.

"Alfonso, it was definitely room 705."

"Juan, there was no one booked into room 705 on Saturday night! I have double checked!"

"But I have the photographs to prove it!"

"Then you will have to let me see them, Juan, and I might recognise them."

"I haven't developed them yet. I was waiting to speak to you first to see if it was worthwhile. I will do it now. Speak to you later."

Juan immediately went into his dark room and started to develop and lighten the photos. He did everything the old fashioned way and didn't like to rush things, but he was desperate to see who he had photographed on Saturday night.

The woman's face had started to materialize first. He didn't recognise her. But as the photograph developed before his very eyes, he was drawn to her hair. It was so straight, shiny and black. He knew that hairstyle! He had seen this woman before, but he couldn't think where.

He now only hoped that he might recognise the man in the photo. If not, he would show the photo to Alfonso, to give him the chance to shed some light on the amorous couple.

Two seconds later he realised he didn't need any help from Alfonso, or anyone else for that matter. The Lord had smiled down upon him. He looked up to the heavens, blessed himself and said, "Thank you Lord!"

He had hit the jackpot!

It wasn't her husband.

The man was Carlos Angel Martinez!

Chapter 21

It was Monday evening and Juan was sitting in his living room, drinking a glass of red wine, Faustino V Reserva-rioja 2004, and looking at the dozen photographs of Carlos Angel Martinez and his lady friend, which he had spread all over his coffee table.

He was thinking of how much money he could make out of these pictures.

Should he blackmail Martinez for all the money he could get out of him, or should he mess up his life by selling them to the newspapers for everyone to see?

'Any of these options would be excellent', he thought to himself as he sipped on his wine.

It didn't take him long to reach his decision.

He had always thought that Martinez owed him, so this was his chance to get some of the money, that he felt was rightfully his, back from that two faced bastard. This was about more than money. This was personal with a capital "P".

This was the big one, the one he had been waiting for, and he didn't really want to share it with anyone, but Alfonso had become a friend as well as informant, so he wasn't going to cut him out of this deal. Besides he still needed someone on the inside as his eyes and ears, as he didn't really know how this was all going to pan out.

He lifted his mobile and dialled Alfonso's number. Alfonso saw Juan's name appear on his phone and answered almost immediately.

"Hello Juan, I'm sorry I haven't called you back, but I still haven't found out who was in room 705."

He is such a nice guy thought Juan as he heard his apologetic tone on the other side of the phone.

"It's ok, I've found out for myself. I've developed the photos."

"Does that mean I am out of the equation?"

"Not at all Alfonso, we are in this together."

"Thanks Juan, that's great news. I thought you were going to tell me that you didn't need me. Do I have to know who is in the photographs?"

"No, you don't. In fact it's probably better that you don't know, in the meantime anyway. If we do this properly, you will be getting a much bigger payout this time, but it will probably be the last."

Alfonso felt a tingle shoot down his spine. A bigger payout than normal! It must be someone rich or famous, or both, he thought to himself.

"What do you want me to do now, Juan?"

"Firstly, just listen for any gossip among the staff at the hotel. Any gossip at all, and report back to me. Secondly, find out which of Mr. Martinez's homes his wife Teresa is staying in at the moment. And thirdly, what's the name of the woman who works in the hotel with the long, straight black shiny hair?"

"Maria Lopez. Why?"

"No reason, I was just being curious. Now don't call me again, until you have some definite information. In fact don't call this number again. I will make contact with you somehow. Adios."

Alfonso sat his mobile down on his desk as a shiver engulfed his whole body. This was becoming deadly serious...heavy duty. It was obvious to him that it was either Mr or Mrs Martinez in those photos, but he didn't know which one it was.

Did he really want to be involved in this?

Was it too close to home?

He pictured himself on a sun bed with a cocktail in his hand, on a golden sandy beach in some exotic foreign land, with a beautiful girl at his side, and he immediately knew the answer.

Yes, he wanted to be involved!

Chapter 22

David and Louise were in Malta that Tuesday morning on board the American Gem, which was berthed at the dockside of Valetta harbour. They had risen early and had breakfast in the Café Carousel, so that they could be among the first to disembark, as they wanted to spend some time visiting a little town called Mdina, not far from Valetta. The ship was due to leave harbour at 2 pm that day. Hence their personal schedule – breakfast at 7 am and disembarkation at 7-45 am.

David had done some research on the internet, and had already found the best way to make the journey to "the silent city" as Mdina was commonly known to both natives and visitors alike. All they had to do was turn right as soon as they got off the ship, and walk along the quayside until they reached the first bus stop, which was actually the starting place of the open air bus tour. They had already done this, and were now waiting at the bus stop, first in the queue.

They were on schedule.

"How many horse and carriages did we pass on the way here?" asked David.

They had walked the gauntlet of tourist guide carriage drivers on the quayside, all offering them different "deals" to choose their horse and carriage for a guided tour of Valetta. It had become a bit monotonous saying 'no' to all the persistent driver/guides.

"There must have been one hundred," said Louise, "and they were all beginning to bug me-----continually asking if we wanted a tour. In fact one of them was so 'in my face' that I nearly slapped him. They don't give you a wink of peace, do they?"

"No they don't," he answered and didn't' say another word.

He could feel her annoyance, but he didn't know the real reason why she was so annoyed.

Deep down she was actually upset that they weren't getting a horse drawn carriage to take them around Valetta before they went to Mdina. She didn't say anything, but once again she felt aggrieved that she couldn't get what she really wanted because of a lack of finance. Then the bus arrived and they paid the thirty euros for the trip, picked up their complimentary earphones, and went up to the top deck to choose their seats. It wasn't long before the bus was full, and they were on their way to firstly Valetta itself, just at the top of the hill, then a town called Mosta, and finally onto Mdina.

It had started to rain just before they had reached Mdina, and the driver immediately stopped the bus and went upstairs and started handing out 'pacamacs' (plastic rain coats) to everyone on the top deck. It wasn't raining much at all, but it was quite windy, so everyone found it quite difficult to unfurl these things and put them on. There were huge howls of laughter as some people found it more difficult than others. Many people also had their cameras out taking photographs.

It was at this point that David felt that feeling for the first time in the trip...the feeling that someone was watching them.

He felt that someone was taking photos of them, but as he looked around the bus at everyone taking pictures, none of the cameras seemed to be pointing their way.

He just shrugged it off as a classic case of paranoia, and didn't mention it to Louise.

They finally reached Mdina at approximately 10-30 am, which gave them about two hours to explore. Mdina is a walled town situated on a hill in the centre of Malta, and has a population of only three hundred. It is a tiny town but it still has a cathedral, (ST Paul's) a large town square, a palace, two chapels, history museum, dungeons, convent and monastery.

This was what attracted David and Louise to this particular town. They found it fascinating!

They walked into the town through a drawbridge with turrets at each side and were met at the other side by a knight in shining armour, a Knight of Malta. They were not disappointed as they walked through the narrow curving streets encased by the high ancient buildings, but both found it rather claustrophobic and slightly creepy in the quieter streets.

After an hour or so they decided to have lunch in the only restaurant they could find.

David ordered some sandwiches and two glasses of red wine.

Louise would have ordered a bottle of the best red. She seemed quiet, so David asked her, "Is anything wrong?"

"No, not at all, I'm just taking in Mdina. It's wonderful, isn't it?"

"Yes I love it. It's like going back in time. It looks just like a film set for a movie about Arthur and the Knights of the Round Table, but I must admit I did feel as if the walls were closing in on us, as we walked through those really narrow streets."

"I'm glad you said that, because that's exactly how I felt. But I actually felt something else."

Louise hesitated, and then continued. "You might think I'm being stupid here David, but I also felt as if someone was watching me. I felt and still feel as if I'm being stalked!"

David didn't say anything at first, but then said, "I don't think you are being silly, but I think it is probably just that claustrophobic feeling that is making you feel like that. Don't worry about it and I'm sure that feeling will go away."

Even as he tried to reassure Louise with his words, he was thinking to himself that it wasn't paranoia on the top deck of that bus.

He had felt exactly the same way, and he didn't have any walls closing in on him.

He had nothing but open skies!

Chapter 23

"What the fuck do you think you are doing? I saw what you did on Sunday! Are you trying to get us beaten up, or even killed?"

Emilio Torres had just entered his Uncle Juan's apartment and walked straight into a vocal blast.

Juan had telephoned Emilio, who was the son of his sister Elisabeth, earlier that morning, and asked him to come round to his flat as he wanted to talk to him about something he couldn't discuss over the telephone.

Juan had a soft spot for him and had always looked out for him as he grew up, but unfortunately he also got him mixed up in the same thieving business as himself, and had even taught him some tricks of the trade when he was a boy. Emilio was now twenty-four years of age, and was indeed a fully-fledged professional thief and pickpocket. However on that Sunday he had done something really silly, and placed Juan in a difficult position.

"Why did you take that couple's bag, outside the Hotel Sants? You know this is not your patch. This patch belongs to the Morales brothers and you know that I work for them. I'm supposed to tell them if I see anyone else working this area, and they mean 'anyone'. You know how evil they can be, don't you?"

"I know Uncle Juan, but it only took two minutes. I was told to be waiting around the corner about midday. I was to stay there until I received a phone call saying that they were waiting outside of the hotel at the taxi rank. All I had to do then was walk around the corner and take the bag. It was easy money."

"How did you know there was money in the bag?"

"I didn't, I don't mean easy money in that respect, although there was one hundred and fifty British pounds in the bag. I was told I could keep any money that was in the bag and I would also be given three hundred euros for doing the job. The only other thing I had to do was to keep my mouth shut! Uncle Juan, I couldn't refuse!"

"Who called you?"

"I honestly don't know."

"What else was in the bag?"

"Just a pair of jeans, a v-neck, a pair of shoes, a new bottle of after shave, two mobile phone chargers and a bottle of perfume."

"That's all. Nothing else?" asked Juan.

"Oh! E-mail documents for their cruise and e-mail tickets for their flight home and hotel booking for two nights after their cruise. That was it!"

"Who paid you?"

"Look, it was a friend of mine, in the business."

"What's his name?"

"You don't know him Uncle Juan!"

"Try me!"

"Eduardo Salgado, but it wasn't him who wanted it done. He was just the go-between.

It was his friend who wanted the job done. That's all there was to it."

"What's the name of the guy who wanted it done? The 'friend of a friend'."

"I can't tell you that. I don't want beaten up. Anyway I don't know his name."

"Don't lie to me Emilio! Do you think I'm stupid?"

"I can't tell you, I promised I wouldn't say a word to anyone!"

"Emilio, have you got your three hundreds euros for doing the job?"

"Yes."

"So you can't lose that. Now I'm going to give you a choice. If you don't tell me the name, then I am going to have to tell the Morales brothers."

"But Uncle Juan, I am family!"

"Family doesn't come into this. This is business! Tell me the name and I will cover for you, and that will be the end of it."

Emilio hesitated, ran his fingers through his hair, and then covered his face with his two hands.

One minute later he blurted out,

"Promise me you won't tell anyone that I told you! And I mean never ever tell anyone! He will kill me if he ever finds out that I told you!"

"I promise."

"Ok, it was the assistant chief of the Mossos d'Esquadra, Senor Gilberto Ramirez."

Chapter 24

"Good morning, can I speak to Senor Carlos Angel Martinez please?"

It was Wednesday morning and Juan wanted to start the ball rolling.

"I'm sorry sir, but Senor Martinez is on holiday at the moment, can I be of assistance?"

"No thank you, I have to speak to him personally."

"Hold on sir, Miss Beverley Parker, his personal assistant is in her office today, she may be able to help you. Do you want me to put you through?"

"Yes please."

"Who shall I say is calling?"

"I would rather not say at this time, could you just put me through to Miss Parker please?"

"Hold the line please."

There was silence at the other end of the line, which gave Juan Marquez time to visualise Miss Beverley Parker in his mind.

She was probably a blonde thirty something, with blue eyes, long legs, teetering on high stiletto heels, with a short skirt and a voluptuous figure. Real eye candy!

She was more than likely still single because she was a career girl with no time for romance, and she hailed from England, if her name was anything to go by.

"Good morning sir, how can I help you?" Her voice sounded a lot older than he had imagined.

That was because Miss Beverley Parker was sixty years of age, always wore her grey hair in a bun, and wore black horn-rimmed spectacles to help her ailing eyesight.

She wore sensible flat shoes and always wore tweed two piece suits, short jacket and long skirt which reached below her knees, no matter the weather--- sun, rain or snow. The only two things that Juan had imagined correctly were that she was indeed single and she was born in England- Slough to be exact, home of the Mars bar.

She had arrived in Spain as a twenty two year old and had liked it so much the she never returned home. She had worked all over Spain but eventually settled in Barcelona and gained employment in the hotel business. She had started working in one of Carlos Angel Martinez's hotels thirty years previous as a receptionist, but had worked her way up through the ranks until Carlos had made her his personal assistant. That was twenty years ago, and now no one got to Carlos without first getting past Miss Parker.

"I would like to speak to Carlos Angel Martinez please, but I believe he is on holiday. Could you give me a contact number that would enable me to get in touch with him?"

Miss Parker just laughed and said, "I'm sorry but that's just not possible, Senor.........?"

She paused and waited for Juan finishing the sentence by giving her his name. Juan didn't oblige but did continue by asking,

"Surely you have his mobile phone number, so that you can contact him in case of any emergency?"

"I do, but I don't think that is any of your business, and I don't think that this is an emergency case, or are you telling me that it is, Senor..........?."

She paused and waited again for a name.

"No, it's not an emergency Miss Parker, it's just that I am only in Barcelona until Monday, and I really did want to speak to Carlos. You see, we were at school together at the convent of the Sisters of La Sagrada Familia and remained great friends for many years after that. I haven't seen him for thirty seven years and I just thought I would look him up."

Juan's story had hit a soft spot somewhere in Miss Parker's body, perhaps her heart if she had one, and her tone of voice changed.

"Actually, I will be speaking to him this afternoon regarding his business. I could pass on your telephone number if you wish. I'm sure he would like to speak to you about old times."

Juan smiled. He had cracked the British Bulldog. She was letting him through her defences.

"That would be fantastic Miss Parker. Do you have a pen ready and I will give you my mobile number."

He read out the phone number of a stolen mobile, which he had acquired from one of his crook friends. He would only use it for this call then throw it away.

"Please tell him that I am really excited about the thought of speaking to him, and that I can't wait to hear his voice again after all these years. Thank you for your help Miss Parker."

"That's not a problem sir, but you still haven't told me your name!"

"Oh... I'm very sorry, it's Juan Marquez."

Miss Parker froze.

When she had first started her job as Senor Martinez's personal assistant, he had told her that if someone named Juan Marquez ever called, either by phone or in person, under no circumstances was he to be allowed through. However within the last year, since he had hopes of becoming Mayor, he had changed his mind completely.

He wanted to know immediately if Juan Marquez tried to make contact.

She knew that she had to adhere to Senor Martinez's instructions, but she also knew deep down, that Juan Marquez was the last person in the world that he wanted to speak to, at his moment in time.

Later that day, at the pre-arranged time, Miss Parker hesitated before she dialled the number. "Good afternoon sir, I hope you are enjoying your holiday. Nothing to report on the business side of things, but you had one personal call."

"Good afternoon Beverley, I hope you are keeping well, and I am glad that everything seems to be running smoothly as far as the business goes. What about this personal call? What's it about, and who called?"

"It was about your school days at the convent, and it was from a gentleman called Juan Marquez."

This time it was Carlos who froze.

Chapter 25

David walked down the gangplank backwards, look-ing into Louise's eyes as she walked towards him. He was singing that old Dean Martin song, 'That's Amore'.

"When the moon hits your eye like a big pizza pie, 'That's amore,'

When the world seems to shine like you've had too much wine, 'That's amore,'

Bells will ring, ting-a- ling a-ling..............."

"David will you stop that racket please. You know you can't sing a note. Are you just trying to annoy me?"

"No, I'm not, I'm trying to get you in the mood for our visit to dear old Napoli."

That's where the ship was docked that Wednesday, at the Stazione Marittima, the large terminal located right in the city centre near the Piazza Municipio.

"Ok, I promise I won't sing another note, if you prom-ise to lighten up and relax, you seem so tense," added David.

"It's your singing that makes me tense, but you've got a deal anyway," and Louise raised her right hand and gave David a high five.

Louise was laughing now and that made David feel really good, as he wasn't too sure about her state of mind at that time. He felt that she had drunk too much the previ-ous evening, as she had said some hurtful things to him and seemed to be trying to start an argument. It was as if she wanted David to fall out with her. He didn't like it when she was acting like that, especially in front of other guests. David hadn't re-acted and just continued his conversation with some of the other people they had met at dinner.

However this morning she looked more like the old Louise, as they walked hand in hand towards Naples city centre.

They could have gone to the beautiful island of Capri, or the lovely city of Sorrento, both of which were located close to Naples. David in fact had suggested that they visit Pompeii, a place he had always wanted to see.

Pompeii was built in the shadows of the volcano Mount Vesuvius, and on August 24th, 79 ad, the volcano erupted and buried the city in ash. Twenty thousand people were killed, but the ancient city was preserved just as it was, seconds before the volcano erupted. Houses, shops, paintings, cups, bottles, tables, chairs, dogs and even people were frozen in time, which allowed future generations a chance to see how people lived two thousand years ago. This fascinated David and he had even worked out, via the internet, exactly how to get there from Naples. Take a taxi to the main train station at Piazza Garibaldi and then the train to the station called Pompeii Scavi, which was situated only yards from the gates to the site of Pompeii itself.

However Louise said that she didn't want to trek around some ancient ruins, which were of no interest to her whatsoever. She was the strongest willed of the two, and so if she decided they weren't going to Pompeii, then that was it----no Pompeii. David was very weak in these situations, and just accepted her decisions. He even made up excuses to support her.

"Yes, it's too hot to walk around the ruins in that blazing sun," he had said, even though they were going to do exactly the same in Naples. But then Louise had suggested that option.

David only stood firm when it came to decisions about their finances.

Naples looked very busy as they walked through the dozens of tour guides all offering different tours of the city, all of which they refused. They only wanted to be left alone, to find their own way around this romantic city. They reckoned they could handle this quite easily.

However they immediately encountered a problem when they reached The Via Cristoforo Colombo, the road that ran along the quayside. The traffic was horrendous, and it took them a full five minutes to cross that one street.

They decided there and then, that they would walk around the city, just taking in the sheer 'Italianess' of it all. They would do some shopping and indeed see what sort of bargains they could pick up—if any. They would walk up and down the narrow streets where the natives stayed, and get a feel for the local people selling fruit and veg from their street stalls in the poorer areas of the city. But they would just have to come back to this street and find a roadside café, where they would have a drink and some lunch and watch these crazy drivers.

That was how they came to find themselves sitting at a terrace table outside Café Mama Rosa on The Via Cristoforo Colombo.

"What would you like to eat, Louise?"

"How about, as this is supposedly the home of pizzas, we share a pizza margherita and a bottle of their best red wine?" answered Louise as the handsome waiter approached. It was then that she did something that David had never seen her do before. She unbuttoned the top two buttons of her blouse to reveal her cleavage. She then grabbed the menu from David, and pointed to the menu to show the waiter what she wanted, knowing all of the time that the waiter couldn't take his eyes of her breasts. David was astounded, but didn't say anything, he just added, "And a half carafe of house red please," as Louise was so busy flirting, that she forgot to order the wine. At least she's relaxed, he thought to himself, and maybe 'this could be my lucky night'.

He answered himself immediately with 'my luck doesn't run that far,' as Louise had ignored him in the bedroom for a long time.

The wine soon arrived and they sat watching the passing traffic as they sipped the lovely house red. The Napolitan drivers were mad, but very entertaining to watch. They parked their cars anywhere. They watched as one driver triple parked his car, and then when the two cars parked on his inside moved away, his car looked as if it had been abandoned in the middle of the road.

David and Louise tucked into their tasty pizza as they smiled and laughed at the antics of the drivers. "Another half carafe please, Alessandro," David shouted to the waiter as he picked up the empty carafe and showed it to him.

"This has been a very enjoyable, entertaining and relaxing day, don't you think Louise?"

"I think it's been great, and it's not finished yet," she answered, as she watched Alessandro pour some wine into her empty glass. She knew once again that he couldn't take his eyes of her. She smiled at him and then David.

David didn't like this. She was playing with him.

She was enjoying the feeling of power that she held over men. The waiter walked away and Louise started to laugh as she pointed out onto the street at a car that had just smashed into the back of the car in front. "There's another crash!"

This was the third bump they had witnessed while they ate lunch. They had also seen one person being hit by a car. It wasn't surprising there were so many crashes or knockdowns, the drivers didn't take any notice of road signs or traffic lights. They ignored them all.

David tried to picture the road from above. He imagined the cars would look like a colony of ants, weaving in and out and around each other, trying to find the quickest route home.

That's where David and Louise were preparing to go now----home, or to the ship to be more precise, which they could see just across the road. It was already five past four.

They paid their bill, leaving a tip for Alessandro and left the café to try and cross the road. Louise gave him a kiss on both cheeks before she left, while at the same time pressing her breasts against his chest. David was embarrassed but didn't say a word. He just walked over to the kerb and stood amongst the throng of people who were all waiting to cross the road.

Although there were hundreds of cars they all seemed to keep moving, in fact some incredibly fast considering the circumstances. David noticed a break in the traffic and decided he would make his move.

It was then that he felt the push on his back.

A second later he was lying in the middle of the busy road. He was lucky.

The driver had seen him and had managed to hit the brakes and stop just in time. The car had hit David, but only slightly. He was a bit dazed but otherwise unhurt. He looked up to see the face of Louise looking at him,

"David, are you alright?" She screamed.

"Yes I'm fine. Help me up."

As Louise helped David back up onto his feet, the driver rushed out of his car, an old and battered Fiat 127, talking so quickly, that David didn't even know what language he was speaking, until he heard him say "Mama Mia." His arms flailed all around him, like the tentacles of an octopus.

"IT'S ALRIGHT I'm not hurt," said David.

Just at that, Alessandro appeared and asked David if he was okay.

"Yes I'm fine thanks, but could you just explain to the driver that I'm not hurt, I don't think he understands me."

"He understands you perfectly sir, it's not you he's worried about. It's his car!"

David's jaw dropped.

He turned, shook his head, and slowly walked to the safety of the pavement on the other side of the road. Louise caught up with him and flung her arms around his neck and kissed him.

"Oh I'm so glad you're not hurt. I got such a terrible fright there when you flashed off the pavement in front of that car."

She held him close and kissed him again.

"I'm okay Louise, I was very lucky. You know what happened, don't you?"

"What do you mean?"

"I was pushed Louise! That's what happened."

"No you couldn't have been! I was standing right behind you!"

That's what worried David. She had been standing right behind him!

Chapter 26

David and Louise still had an hour before they had to be back on board ship, and he decided that he needed a dram to settle his nerves before he went anywhere. They went into a small bar about fifty yards down the road and picked a small table for two, which was just below a huge picture of Diego Maradonna—a legend in Naples. Louise offered to go to the bar, something that she never did, but David said he would go, he was fine.

"What do you want to drink?"

"I'll have a gin and bitter lemon with plenty of ice please."

David approached the bar, at the same time checking if they had any malt whiskies displayed on the gantry. He could see only one. Fortunately it was Glenmorangie 10 year old, one that he liked. He ordered up both drinks and the barman soon returned and asked David what he wanted in his whisky. David tutted and replied, "A true Scotsman doesn't take anything in his whisky, except maybe a little water, but nothing for me thanks."

The barman smiled and placed the glass of whisky on the bar. David lifted both drinks and made his way across to the table, but he had an eerie feeling that someone was watching him.

Suddenly he realised that he was right!

Someone was watching his every move!

It was Diego Maradonna. The eyes on that huge picture seemed to be looking straight at him, following him across the room. He smiled, sat down, handed the gin and bitter lemon to Louise, and then took a sip of his malt. The subtle taste of honey with a delicate hint of nuts soothed his taste buds and a warm glow overwhelmed his whole body. At that precise moment, there seemed to be no one in the room but him.

He was in a trance, a Glenmorangie trance.

"I think you should go and see the ship's doctor when we get back on board."

Louise's voice sounded so distant, but it did snap him out of his elevated state.

"I don't need to, I'm fine. I saw the car coming even though it happened so quickly, and I 'went with it.' I rolled across the bonnet and landed easily on the ground. I've got a scratch on my elbow and that's all." He showed the cut on his elbow to Louise.

"I just wish I could get my hands on the bastard who pushed me!"

Louise looked a little shocked. "David, I didn't see anyone pushing you."

"Look Louise, I know when someone pushes me!"

She could see the anger, and suspicion in his eyes. She waited a minute before adding,

"There were so many people waiting to cross the road, maybe someone accidentally bumped into you."

David sipped his malt, calmed himself down, and after a few seconds conceded that she might be right. "Maybe you're right. I was just so angry. I could have been killed!"

"I know," Louise answered sympathetically, "but the most important thing is that you are alright!"

David knowingly nodded his head as he finished the last drops of his malt. He felt a warm glow deep in his chest. Louise had already finished her drink and suggested they return to the 'Gem'.

They left the bar via the back door, and as soon as they were outside, Louise stopped and pushed David up against the wall and rubbed herself against him.

"You like this, don't you?"

David didn't reply. He just stood there.

Louise opened his shirt buttons and put her two hands inside, rubbing his back and chest. She opened her own blouse and unclipped her bra, before pushing her naked breasts against his bare torso. David looked left and right. For god's sake, anyone could see them, they were standing right beside the bar car park.

Then Louise kissed him and said,

"Why don't we go back to the ship, get changed and go out early to one of the ship's posh restaurants? You can get changed first and go down to one of the bars. How many are there?"

"Seventeen," David managed to say in between breaths.

"You can book a table at the Grand Mirage, have a nice relaxing drink while I change into something sexy, and then I'll come and get you! We'll then go and share a lovely meal, have some cocktails and see what the night brings! How does that sound?"

"That sounds brilliant, just what I was going to suggest!" David added jokingly.

Louise kissed him, and leaned back closing her buttons at the same time. She handed her bra to David, which he stuffed into his pocket after re-buttoning his own shirt.

They walked away hand in hand, and David thought to himself that this indeed could be his lucky night. He just hoped that the bra in his pocket didn't set off the metal detector that they had to pass through when re-boarding ship.

How would he explain that?

Chapter 27

"What did he say? Did he sound aggressive or angry? You didn't give him my phone number, did you?" Carlos sounded agitated.

"No sir. I told him that you were on holiday but I would be speaking to you today, and that I would pass on his phone number if he wished. I have it here. As for sounding angry, he actually sounded the opposite. He was very pleasant. He said that he was really excited about hearing your voice again, and catching up on old times. That was it really sir."

"Where was he calling from?"

"Barcelona. He said that he would be there until Monday."

"Where is he staying?"

"He didn't say sir, and the number he gave me was for a mobile phone."

"Okay Beverley, give me the number."

Carlos took a note of the number and then said his goodbyes to Beverley.

He poured himself a glass of red wine and stood looking at the notepad on which he had written the name Juan Marquez and the mobile phone number. He finished his wine then lifted the telephone.

'Now is as good a time as any' he thought, and dialled the number!

Chapter 28

"Could I speak to Juan Marquez please?"

"Speaking... is that you Carlos?"

"Yes it is, Juan, it's so good to hear from you after all this time. How are you keeping?"

Carlos didn't know what to expect from Juan, but his voice sounded quite pleasant.

"I'm feeling great, thanks Carlos. Thanks for returning my call so quickly, I believe you're on holiday?"

"Yes, I'm on a cruise, but when Beverley called and said you had phoned, I just had to find out what you wanted to talk about."

"Nothing in particular," he lied, "I am on holiday myself in Barcelona, and I thought we could meet up and talk about old times."

That's what Carlos was worried about....old times.

"Do you mean like the time at the convent, when sister Marie tried to chase us on her bike, but we had let her tyres down, and she fell off!" said Carlos.

"Yes, remember that. What about the times when we used to go into that candy shop and steal sweets," added Juan.

"Or what about the time when we were trying to run away from the convent, and you ripped your pants on the fence, and we had to go back because you needed another pair!" laughed Carlos.

Juan laughed and found himself really enjoying their reminiscing, but that was not the real reason for his call.

Carlos on the other hand was quite happy with the lightness of the conversation, but decided to change tact a little. "Where do you live now Juan?"

Juan was a great liar and immediately replied, "I stay in Seville. I have lived there for thirty years. I never married so I don't have any family. The only family I ever had was our pickpocket gang all those years ago. However that was a long time ago. What about you, Carlos? I know that you have done very well for yourself in the hotel business, married Teresa, have a son called Miguel, and that you are campaigning to become Mayor of Barcelona."

Carlos was getting a little worried, as it was obvious Juan had done more than a little research on him and his family.

"That's right, and what type of business are you in Juan?"

"I'm in photography."

"How did you get involved in that?"

Carlos was trying to keep the conversation as upbeat and friendly as possible, but he was beginning to detect an aggressive tone in Juan's voice.

"Well, remember when you dumped me on the steps of Barcelona Cathedral?"

Carlos stopped breathing momentarily.

"One of the priests who helped me kick my drugs habit, enrolled me in a photography course and I've never looked back. I now have my own digital photography processing business."

"That's great," said Carlos hesitantly.

"That's the reason I called you, Carlos."

The punchline---- thought Carlos.

"I have some photographs I think you might be interested in."

"Oh? And why would that be Juan? Are they old photos?"

"No, they are very recent photographs of you and another woman."

"What do you mean, 'another woman'?"

"I mean that the woman is not your wife, and she is naked!"

"You must have made some kind of mistake, Juan."

"No mistake, Carlos. Maybe this will jog your memory. Saturday night. The Hotel Sants, Barcelona. Does that ring any bells?"

It certainly did....alarm bells! Carlos didn't know what to say.

"How do I know they are not fake photos, after all you are an expert on digital photograph processing, aren't you?"

"I can assure you, they are genuine, and the good news is that they are for sale. So you have a choice. You can buy these photographs directly from me, or I can sell them to the media. I'm sure they would be interested. I can e-mail or fax you a sample of the merchandise if you are interested. In the meantime I will give you another phone number so that you can contact me, but don't take too long!"

Carlos couldn't believe what was happening as he fumbled with his pen, while scribbling down the new number.

"How much do you want for these photos?"

"One million euros!"

"But that's just blackmail."

"Yes it is," said Juan as he pressed the end call button.

Chapter 29

Carlos poured himself a whisky and water, he needed something stronger than wine this time. He sat down and considered what his next move should be. He had thought about this moment many times over the years, and it hadn't really bothered him.

'I will cross that bridge when I come to it' he had always thought.

But now that it was actually here, he didn't know what to do!

Should he just ignore Marquez, and wait and see what he would do next.

Should he phone him back right now and ask him to fax the pictures so that he could see them for himself.

Should he just phone his 'fixer', the guy who could fix anything. This would be right up his street. 'No, that will be my last resort', he thought to himself.

He decided to take the second option, and dialled the number.

"Marquez, I want to see the pictures. Fax them to me. There's no way I'm giving you my e-mail address!"

Carlos then read out the fax number and waited for Juan to say something.

"Marquez, are you still there?"

"Yes I'm here."

"When are you going to fax them?"

"I'll fax them just now, but something else has come up."

"What are you talking about, Marquez. I thought you only wanted to 'sell' me those pictures?"

"I do, but I now have something else in my possession that I think is somehow connected, but I just can't work it out. I have a small black luggage bag that was stolen from a Scottish couple on Sunday, while they waited for a taxi outside your Hotel Sants. Do you know anything about that?"

Carlos hesitated before replying,

"I was told of the theft simply because it had taken place outside of my hotel. I don't like to hear of anything being stolen inside or around any of my hotels. That sort of thing can lead to a hotel getting a bad reputation."

"Well I think there is more to it, Carlos, but I'm going to forget about it for now. But I want you to know I'm working on it, because I know that more times than not, when Gilberto Ramirez is involved in something like this, you are usually behind it. I'll fax the pictures immediately. Just don't take too long to get back to me!"

Carlos said nothing. This was one of those times when silence was the best policy, but he couldn't help thinking how the hell Marquez could have found out that Ramirez had something to do with the theft.

Chapter 30

A single photograph appeared one minute later.

He poured himself another whisky as he watched it slowly roll off the fax machine. Even from this grainy black and white fax picture, he could easily recognise himself along with a woman with long, straight, black hair. She was topless. She had him pinned back against the wall. He had no shirt on.

How on earth had Marquez managed to get these pictures?

It didn't matter now, how he had got them. The fact of the matter was that he did have them, and that he was going to blackmail him because of them.

This was not a good situation.

He would have to get it 'fixed'. He had no choice.

He lifted the phone and dialled the 'Fixer's' number.

Chapter 31

Gilberto Ramirez was at home when his mobile rang.

"We have a problem!" The voice at the other end started.

"What's wrong Carlos?"

"I've had a phone call from a man from my distant past. He has photographs of me with a woman—not my wife—in a compromising situation. He wants to 'sell' them to me, if you know what I mean. Not only that, he says he has in his possession the bag that was stolen from the Scottish couple, outside the Hotel Sants on Sunday."

"He is lying about that, Carlos, because the guy who stole it returned it to the hotel. That was the plan. I told him he could take any money that was in the bag, but to make sure the bag was returned, minus all the travel documents. He was to say that he had found the bag up a side street, and as there was a Hotel Sants baggage ticket attached, he was returning it in the hope that there would be a reward. He did that this morning."

Carlos felt a glimmer of hope as he thought if Marquez could lie about that, then maybe he was lying about the photos. That glimmer only lasted a milli-second as he looked at the faxed picture in his hand.

"He might not be telling the truth about the bag, but he's certainly not lying about the photos. They're definitely for real. And he said something else about you Gilberto. He knew you were behind the bag theft."

Gilberto felt anger brewing in the pit of his stomach.

Eduardo Salgado or Emilio Torres must have talked. One of them had opened their big mouth. The Fixer now had a problem of his own to fix!

"Who is this man, and where does he stay?" asked Gilberto.

"He's someone I knew when I was younger, but I haven't seen or heard from him for thirty seven years. Now he appears out of the blue with these photos to blackmail me, but I don't know where he is staying, all I can tell you is that he is holidaying in Barcelona. It will be like looking for a needle in a haystack!"

"Carlos, don't panic, just give me his name and I'll do my best to try and find him."

"Okay Gilberto, his name is Juan Marquez."

Gilberto laughed out loud. He couldn't believe the name Carlos had just given him.

"Carlos, he stays in an apartment straight across from your Hotel Sants, and has done so for the past fifteen years. He is the named witness regarding the bag theft on Sunday. His nephew is Emilio Torres, the thief who stole the bag. Everything fits. As for the photos, don't worry about them, I'll fix it."

Carlos then remembered why he called Gilberto 'the Fixer'.

Chapter 32

Civitavecchia, the gateway to Rome as far as cruise ships are concerned, is located fifty miles west-north-west of the capital itself, and this is where they found themselves on that beautiful Thursday morning. They were both lying on sun beds at poolside on deck fifteen when they should really have been in the 'eternal city', Rome.
But yesterday had been a long day.

David had been knocked down in Naples, and at the time, he really thought Louise had pushed him off the kerb into the path of an on coming car, the driver of which was a maniacal Napolitan who had ranted loudly at David. Louise really had been acting strangely since the start of the holiday, he thought, but surely she wasn't capable of that.

Anyhow things had changed after that incident and they both had a wonderful evening, well what he could remember of it!

By the time they had returned to the ship from Naples, Louise had decided that she needed perfume, as the bottle she had bought in duty free had been in the bag, which was stolen in Barcelona.

"Why don't you go up and get changed and go and book a table for dinner, and then you can go to one of the bars and have a nice drink. In fact why don't I meet you later in the Malt Bar?"

The Malt bar was a Scottish themed pub with a great selection of malt whiskies.

"Either that or you can come with me just now." Louise had added.

"Where are you going?"

"I'm going shopping at the ship's shopping mall."

"Try saying that with a few drinks in you!" David had joked, before adding, "No, I don't like the sound of that. I'll go with your first suggestion and meet you in the Malts! See you later!"

As David had skipped away from Louise, he had found himself singing along with the piped music coming from the bar's music system, 'Luck be a lady tonight' from the musical 'Guys and Dolls'. He had thought that music was appropriate because that's the way his night seemed to be going.

'This is going to be a great night!' He had thought to himself.

Half an hour later he could be found sitting at a table in the dimly lit corner of the Malts Bar, with a glass of Auchentoshan 10 year old in front of him. He had taken his first sip and was so chilled out, that he could have gone to sleep. He was glad that he had decided to book the table for dinner first, because now, he could just sit there at his homely table next to the real log fire, and just float away.

Louise had appeared about seven malts later.

She was wearing a black low cut corset with diamante decoration, and a black pencil skirt, which reached down to her calves. To finish her outfit she was wearing black patent high heels. She was stunning! David was anticipating what might happen later on in the evening and that song; 'Luck be a lady' had darted back into his mind. He had hummed it as they had made their way to the Grand Mirage restaurant on deck seven, where they were immediately met by the table coordinator who fed their names into the computer, which flagged up their table number. He then paged their personal waiter who escorted them to their table. It was very well organised.

They had been served by Christian who came from Bogotá, the capital of Columbia, South America. He looked about twenty five years old, about five feet eight, pale skinned, (not what David and Louise had expected a Columbian to look like), and had dark brown hair, which he continually fed around his ears with his index finger to flow down onto the top of his shoulders. Although it was quite long he kept it very neat. He was a bit of a looker Louise had remarked to David. He looked immaculate in his black shiny shoes, black trousers, white shirt, and yellow and black pinstripe waistcoat. He spoke perfect English with an American accent, which he had told them was because he was self-taught, as he had learned the language by watching hundreds of American movies. He had been a great waiter and very entertaining. David could remember giving him a twenty-dollar tip.

However lying on his sun bed that next morning he couldn't even remember what he had eaten for dinner that previous evening, but he could remember Louise encouraging him to "have another drink".

He also remembered that they had gone on to the disco club after their meal and dancing to the Killer's song 'Human'.

He had burned up that dance floor, he thought to himself, as he lay there suffering from a massive hangover. He could remember leaving the disco with Louise and making their way along the long corridors of the ship, which seemed to be rather longer last night.

It was coming back to him now.

They were heading back to their room from the club, when Louise had suggested one for the road, in the Champagne bar. They had gone in there and had made conversation with an elderly American couple from Boston. After two glasses of champagne, David had decided it was time for bed and had suggested so to Louise. She had immediately agreed.

David had thought that strange at the time, normally she would argue and say that she wasn't ready to go to bed. They had gone back to their room at 1-00 a.m. as David had thought, although the actual time had only been 11-30 pm.

It had been a long day for him.

Lying at the poolside he believed that they had made love and then gone to sleep, but in truth he couldn't remember. As he lay there with a pounding headache in the hot burning sun, he wondered why Louise wasn't angry this morning.

She had been desperate to see the city of Rome and had talked about it incessantly. David had been frightened to say to her that he could not go to Rome that day. He had blamed it on the fact that he was 'sore all over' due to the knockdown.

"I feel as if I have gone ten rounds with Mike Tyson," he had said. But the real reason was that he had a terrible hangover. He knew that she knew the real reason. He couldn't fool her that easily. But she had surprised him and had accepted it all so calmly!

Why did she seem so content today, lying on her sunbed drinking a pina colada?

How could she drink that pina colada after all she had drunk yesterday? Little sparks of memory darted into David's brain. She had encouraged him to drink. She had suggested him going to the Malt bar by himself before dinner. She had suggested the club, but only had a couple of drinks because she was 'too busy dancing'. She had suggested the Champagne Bar, but didn't drink anything because they didn't serve gin. She had ordered the wine at dinner, but didn't want any herself.

She hadn't drank that much!

Then the final bolt of memory pierced his brain.

He had awakened in the middle of the night.

He had instinctively looked at the digital alarm clock at the side of the bed. It was 4-30 a.m.

There was an empty space beside him where Louise should have been.

He called out her name- no answer.

Louise wasn't there.

Chapter 33

David lay back on his sun bed, his eyes closed behind his dark sunglasses. Every time he moved his head, he could feel his brain reverberate inside his skull. 'Never again' he thought as he inwardly cursed his hellish hangover while he took off his sunglasses to reveal red bleary eyes, and turned round to look at Louise. Her sun bed was set in the upright position, as she sat there elegantly sipping her pina colada. David lay back down, put his sunglasses on and looked straight up at the blue cloudless sky.

'How can I ask Louise where she went at half past four this morning without causing an argument?' he thought to himself. He found himself answering his own question.

'I'll just ask her!'

He slowly sat up on his sun bed, all the while considering how he should start the conversation. "I don't feel too good. How are you feeling this morning?"

Louise sat her drink down on the small table by her side and answered,

"I bet you don't feel any worse than I did at four o'clock this morning."

David once again lay back down on his sun bed as Louise continued talking. He didn't know whether to lie down or sit up. He felt sick.

"I felt terrible. In fact I felt so bad that I got up and went for a walk on deck. I came up to deck fifteen and sat at the poolside. It's surprising how many people are up and about at that time in the morning. After some fresh air I felt a lot better and I went back to bed."

David felt ashamed. He asked her if she was feeling alright now, just closed his eyes and chastised himself for being so suspicious of Louise. His sick feeling had gone.

Louise knew that David got up every morning about four a.m. to go to the toilet. He was as regular as clockwork. She had guessed that last night would have been no different and therefore said that she had left the room about that time.

In reality, she had left the room at one o'clock and returned at half past five.

Chapter 34

Juan Marquez was becoming impatient. He was sitting on his balcony sipping black coffee, looking out across to the Hotel Sants. It was Friday morning and Martinez still hadn't called him back. He stared at the mobile phone on the table, the number of which he had given to Carlos, and willed it to ring. He then looked down onto the street and noticed Alfonso entering the hotel, rushing as usual. He waited ten minutes and then dialled Alfonso's number, hoping that he might have some information for him.

"Buenos Dias Alfonso, anything for me?"

"Buenos Dias Juan, I was beginning to think you had forgotten all about me."

"No not at all, it's just that I've been very busy. Have you found out anything about where Senora Martinez is staying at the moment?"

"Yes she's actually gone to Madrid to visit her son and his family. She should be gone at least two weeks. Senor Martinez is in Seville on business. That's all I could find out."

"Who told you that Senor Martinez is in Seville?"

"The hotel manager told me. Why? Have you heard different?"

"Yes. I was told he was on holiday, and that he would return on Sunday. Anyhow it doesn't really matter now, everything is in hand. We just have to sit and wait. Speak to you soon. Adios."

"Juan! Before you go there was one other thing. You know that a bag was stolen from a Scottish couple outside of the hotel last Sunday, don't you? Yes? Well it was handed into reception on Wednesday morning."

"Why should that be of any interest to me, Alfonso?"

"Because your nephew Emilio handed it in! Emilio Torres."

"Thanks Alfonso. Adios."

Juan couldn't get off the phone quick enough. What was Emilio playing at?

There was only one way to find out!

Chapter 35

Juan lifted his phone and dialled Emilio's number.

"Buenos Dias, is that you Elisabeth? Can I speak to Emilio, please?" said Juan, trying to hide his anger.

A strange voice answered. "I'm sorry but can I ask who is calling?"

Juan was confused and checked the number he had dialled, which was still on the phone screen.

It was the correct number.

"It's his uncle, Juan. Can I ask who I'm speaking to?"

"It's Gabrielle, one of the neighbours."

"If Emilio isn't there can I speak to Elisabeth please?"

"I'm sorry but she can't come to the phone just now. She is too upset."

Juan could hear his heart beating against the walls of his chest. He instinctively knew why she was upset, but he still had to ask. Deep down he knew it was Emilio.

"What do you mean, too upset. What's happened? Is it Emilio?" All his anger had gone.

"Yes. Haven't you heard? Emilio was killed in a car crash in the early hours of this morning."

Silence.

Juan could no longer hear his heart beating.

He could not hear a single sound.

"Tell Elisabeth that her brother Juan will be there in ten minutes."

Chapter 36

Juan found himself sitting beside his sister ten minutes later. She was sitting on a three seater sofa, handkerchief in hand, sobbing uncontrollably.

"What happened, Elisabeth?"

"I don't know. The police have told me that he was driving from Barcelona to Sitges along the coast road and he somehow lost control of the car. That's all I know."

She stopped to try and regain her composure. Her eyes looked red and sore as she wiped them with her sodden handkerchief. One minute later she continued with her terrible tale of woe.

"They think he might have been going too fast, and went through the crash barrier on one of the bad bends along that stretch of road. They think his brakes might have failed."

She paused for a second then said, "Why him? He was a good boy." She started crying again, this time even louder.

Juan put his right arm around his sister's shoulder and squeezed. He didn't know what to say. He waited a moment, and then asked his next question.

"Was there anyone else in the car with him?"

"Yes, his friend, Eduardo Salgado."

Juan tried not to show the shock that stiffened his whole body, but he immediately recognised that name as the 'go between' Emilio had told him about.

He couldn't help but think this was more than just a tragic accident.

Chapter 37

Half an hour later Juan was back in his own apartment, sitting at the table on his balcony. He found himself once again staring at the mobile phone. He was in a state of disbelief. He couldn't believe he would never see Emilio again. It was only two days ago that Emilio was sitting at this very table talking to him, and now he was gone.

He couldn't help but think that it was his fault that Emilio was dead. He felt guilty that the last time he had spoken to him, he had screamed at him, forcing Emilio to tell him about the bag theft. He couldn't get Emilio's words out of his mind.

"He will kill me if he ever finds out that I told you!"

Just then, the mobile phone buzzed. It was Martinez. Juan wiped away the tears from his eyes and answered. "About time too, Martinez!"

"Marquez, I need to see the other photographs. How many do you have?"

"I have twelve in total. You will get them all, as soon as I have my million euros. You will have your photos and that will be the end of it. I promise you."

"How do I know I can trust you, Marquez?"

"Because I have just had some bad news, and as soon as this deal is done I'm leaving Spain forever. You have my word!"

Juan didn't want to have this conversation at this time. His mind was on Emilio.

There was a pregnant pause before Martinez answered.

"You have a deal. Someone will contact you to set up a time and a meeting place for the hand-over. Do you agree?"

"I agree that someone can contact me. Use this number again, it's untraceable anyway. But I will decide the time and place for the hand-over! DO YOU AGREE?" There was anger in his voice.

"I agree Marquez, but I don't want to hear your voice again! Ever! Do you hear me? Adios."

Carlos didn't know if he could trust him, but then again it didn't really matter. The Fixer had only told him to contact Marquez to tell him that he would accept his offer..... all of the photos in exchange for one million euros.

He could remember the Fixer's last words.

'You set up the deal and I will do the rest'

Chapter 38

Maria was stationed at the reception desk as usual on that Friday afternoon. She was finishing work at two o'clock, so she was in a happy and upbeat mood. It was her weekend off and she was really looking forward to it. She wouldn't need to set foot in the Hotel Sants until Monday afternoon at one o'clock. It had been six months since the last time she had managed to get a full weekend off.

What a feeling, and she intended to enjoy every minute of it! It wasn't because she hated her job, in fact the opposite was true. She really loved her work. She liked helping people. But she was so looking forward to chilling out for nearly three whole days.

Maria Lopez was thirty nine years old and had worked in the Hotel Sants for the last six years. She had never married, although she had been asked twice, which was no surprise because she was a stunner. She had beautiful aqua blue eyes with long black eyelashes. When she looked at you, she made you feel as if you were the only one in the room. She had a lovely naturally tanned complexion, high cheekbones, luscious full lips and gleaming white teeth. Her hair was long, black, straight and shining, with a fringe which stopped just above her eyebrows. She had tried to get into the modelling business years earlier, but she had been prevented by her height. She was only five feet four, and that was considered too small.

After that rejection she had thrown herself into her work, and that's how she found herself working in the hotel business.

She was a very conscientious worker and that's why with only two minutes left of her shift, there was no way she was leaving before she had contacted the offices of Assistant Chief Ramirez. She had programmed her computer the previous Sunday to flag up the names, David and Louise Telfer, to remind her to telephone him, if the report he had promised had not arrived at the hotel by Friday. It hadn't arrived.

Now she was off work until Monday and would miss the couple arriving back at the hotel on Sunday. She had been there, when Senor Ramirez had promised the Telfers that he would have that report ready for them when they arrived back at the hotel post cruise. She felt responsible for that. In fact she was the only member of staff who showed any interest in the incident at all. But that was just the way she was. She liked to see things through. She also wanted to tell him that the bag had actually been returned to the hotel on Wednesday morning.

She dialled his direct number, and after several rings Senor Ramirez answered.

"Buenas dias, Senor Ramirez. It's Maria from the Sants hotel. I was just wondering if you have finished that report you were writing, regarding the theft of the Telfer's bag outside our hotel last Sunday. I know you are a busy man, but you did tell them that you would have it ready for them on their return."

"And I shall, Maria. I haven't forgotten about it, it's just that I've been a very busy man over the last few days. I shall have it ready for Sunday. Now is there anything else I can help you with?"

"No, not really, but I just wanted to let you know also, that the bag was actually returned to this hotel on Wednesday morning."

"I know. Now, is that all Maria?"

Maria was surprised at his answer. How did he know that the bag had been returned?

"Did you speak to Juan Marquez?"

"No. I decided against it. He isn't a very reliable witness. Now, is that all?"

Maria didn't like his tone, so she called it a day.

"Yes sir. Thanks for your time. Adios."

Maria put the phone down, and decided that she couldn't really argue with his assessment that Juan Marquez wasn't a reliable witness. That much was true. But he was the only witness they had.

As she left the hotel to go and enjoy her weekend, Maria couldn't help thinking that this was a strange case. Even from the very start.

Senor Ramirez, Assistant Chief of the Mossos d'Esquadra, had arrived at the hotel within minutes of the theft.

He was personally writing the report for insurance purposes, and he knew that the bag had been returned to the hotel. She hadn't told him, and neither had anyone else from the hotel.

Maria reached the end of the street and went into the Café Magic for a coffee. As she sat there she couldn't help but think that Senor Ramirez seemed to be too heavily involved in such a trivial incident.

'There must be more to this case than meets the eye' thought Maria, as she sipped her cappuccino.

Part 2

Chapter 39

The cruise was over, and David and Louise were making their way back to the Hotel Sants for the remainder of their holiday. They were looking forward to two days in Barcelona. In particular David was desperate to visit the Nou Camp Stadium, home of the famous Barcelona football club. As a youngster he had dreamed of playing for them, in front of 120,000 screaming fans. Louise on the other hand, just wanted to visit as many places of interest as possible, and take in the unique atmosphere of one of Europe's most beautiful and vibrant cities.

The previous two days they had enjoyed visits to Livorno and Cannes. In Livorno they had taken the port bus to the town centre, and had sauntered along the main street, window shopping. Friday was also market day, so the back streets were full of market stalls selling all sorts of bric-a-brac. At one of the stalls David had noticed a small luggage bag, which he bought to replace the stolen one, after getting the stall holder to drop his price to six euros. He loved to haggle. They then had a drink at one of the cafes on the busy main thoroughfare, and just watched the world go by. It had been a very relaxing day.

On the Saturday they had been to Cannes and loved every moment of their visit. Although they had liked Livorno, because they had enjoyed such a chilled out day, Cannes was different. It was special. From the second they had disembarked the small tender boat and hit La Croisette, the boulevard that ran along the beautiful sea front, they had been in holiday heaven. There had been so much to see. They had taken a ride on the small tourist train which took them all around Cannes on a two hour journey, from the flash designer shops on La Croisette, like Versace, Chanel and Dolce & Gabbana, to the small shops in the back streets selling all kinds of fresh fish. From the Palais des Festivals to the church of Notre-Dame de l'Esprance at the top of the Suquet hill, the Suquet being the old town. This had been one of their favourite parts of the tour. The view from there had been magnificent, breathtaking, and unforgettable.

They both also had enjoyed going to the Palais des Festivals, home of the Cannes film festival. David had really liked seeing the hand prints of the famous film stars which adorned the pavement tiles outside of the front entrance. Louise had taken a photograph of him placing his hand in the print of Gregory Peck, one of his favourite actors from his younger days. She also took a snap of him with his arm around the shoulder of a metal cut-out of George Clooney.

David didn't want to leave. He was a film lover.

Finally they had walked along La Croisette to the world famous Carlton Hotel, situated on the sea front. They had just stood and looked at this magnificent build-ing, home to the stars during the film festival. David had googled it before the holiday and had tried to impress Louise by telling her that the hotel had even named some of its suites on the 7th floor after some famous actors, like Sean Connery and Sofia Loren.

"They filmed some of the scenes in 'To Catch a Thief' in that hotel," David had said in a final attempt to impress Louise, but it was no use. She didn't even know the film. It didn't matter, it had been a wonderful day, and as they sat in one of the promenade cafes looking out to the sea, Louise sipped her gin and said,

"I will definitely be back here one day, if God spares me. This is wonderful."

David was surprised to hear her use that phrase 'if God spares me.' He had never heard her using that expres-sion before. She looked as if her mind was somewhere else, floating in space, as she lifted her head and looked up to the blue skies. David sipped his small beer and answered,

"I will bring you back for your fiftieth birthday. Would you like that?"

Louise didn't even seem to hear him. Seconds later she turned and looked at him, and finally said, "That would be nice." She didn't even smile. "But I have a horrible feeling that something bad is going to happen to me. I still feel as if I'm being followed!"

David hadn't replied, but he was worried about her.

Chapter 40

They decided that they would not go directly to the hotel as check-in time was 2pm, so they hailed one of the taxis parked outside the port terminal and asked the driver to take them to Las Ramblas. It was now 11 am and they wanted something to eat, as they had skipped an early morning breakfast, so David asked the driver if he could recommend a nice café where they could have brunch. That's how they found themselves sitting on the terrace of the Café Barca, on the Las Ramblas boulevard. They both ordered cheese and bacon paninis and a carafe of house red wine. After ordering, David tied both their cases to the chairs they were sitting on. He hadn't forgotten about their experience the last time they had set foot in Barca.

They sipped their wine and watched the throngs of people walking up and down Las Ramblas. They both loved people watching. They watched the street acts as they performed on the pavement, directly in front of their table. Jugglers, dancers, acrobats and magicians, to name but a few, and they had front row seats.

"You would have to pay good money to see this in a theatre, wouldn't you?" David quipped.

"Yes, this is brilliant," answered Louise as she put a five euro note in the plate that the most recent performer was passing around the tables. He was one of a very talented troupe of acrobats. They had been particularly good.

Before they knew it, it was four o'clock. The time had flown in. They decided they would go to the hotel, check-in, and then have a siesta before dinner. Dinner would be in the hotel, on the chill out terrace which was on the roof, next to the swimming pool. They wouldn't be going out that night, as they had already drank two and a half carafes of wine and were feeling the effects, as well as being a little tired.

"We'll have a relaxing night tonight and we will do all the sightseeing tomorrow. Agreed?" asked David.

"Good idea. I want to see everything tomorrow. Now let's go."

David untied the cases, and passed the smaller one to Louise, with the handle already extended. He pulled out the handle of his own case, and then put his arm around Louise's shoulder. They both walked up the slight incline of Las Ramblas heading towards the Place de Catalunya, where they planned to get a taxi to the Hotel Sants.

"That's me fed and watered. I feel GREAT and I'm ready for anything that life throws at me!" laughed David, as he raised both his hands to the heavens, and looked up to the skies.

Just as well, because life was about to give him one big problem to deal with!

Chapter 41

David and Louise got up early the next morning ready for their day of sightseeing. Well at least David was ready, but Louise was in a nasty mood. David didn't know the reason why. As usual, he remained very placid and asked her if she wanted room service to bring up a breakfast for her.

"No" she snapped. "Just go and find out where we can get the tourist bus!"

"Okay. I'll go down to reception and find out. Do you want anything else brought back up?"

"No. Just get a move on!"

He made his way downstairs to find out about the bus, and was delighted to find Maria was working that morning. She was supposed to be starting at one o'clock that afternoon, but the manager had phoned and asked her to cover for Alfonso, who had called in sick. She didn't mind. She had been off all weekend, and had re-charged her batteries, so she was raring to go. She was also looking forward to see David's face when she gave him his stolen bag back.

"Good morning Maria, it's so nice to see you again. You're looking great as usual. When did you start wearing spectacles? You really suit them."

"Thank you David, that's very kind of you to say so. As for the spectacles, they are fashion glasses. I have ten different pairs to go with different outfits that I wear."

"So the actual glass is clear?" asked David.

"Exactly!"

Maria was wearing a short black skirt, black high heels and a white blouse that seemed to cling to her ample bosom. Her black rimmed glasses with a small white square motif on each arm certainly finished off her sexy outfit.

"I have some good news for you David. Someone handed in your stolen bag. That has never happened before. You will have to check it, to find out if anything is missing." She handed him the bag. David was taken aback. He never expected to see that bag again. He unzipped it to find that everything was still there apart from the money and the travel documents, even the after shave and perfume.

"Who handed it in? Did you get his name and address? I would like to reward him."

"Emilio Torres. He gets the name of being a thief, but I don't know if that is true. I do not have his address but I do have his phone number. Would you like me to call him for you, and ask him to meet you here?"

"Yes that would be great. Can you try just now, before I go out?"

"Certainly, take a seat, and I will try in a few minutes, after I finish this check-in."

David sat down on one of the bright orange chairs and waited for Maria to finish with her guests. Every now and again he would look over at her. He couldn't help staring. She was so attractive. Once she caught him looking, and he felt really embarrassed but she just looked back at him over the top of her sexy glasses and smiled. He felt great.

Maria finished checking in her guests and lifted the telephone. David could hear her talking in Spanish, and reckoned that she was talking to Emilio Torres. She put the phone down and waved him over to the desk. She looked shocked. "That was Emilio's mother."

"Good. Is she going to get in touch with him?"

"No, she can't."

"Then why did he give that phone number?"

"It's the correct phone number. He was killed in a road accident in the early hours of Friday morning."

Chapter 42

Just then Louise came out of the elevator and stormed towards David.

"What do you think you are doing?" she screamed at him. "You left me sitting up in that room by myself half an hour ago. You were supposed to come back up and get me, after you found out where to catch the tourist bus." The bellboy, concierge and Maria stared at her in disbelief, she was shouting like a mad woman. She took no notice of them or the other guests who were sitting in the foyer, as she continued her rant.

"Instead of that, I come down to find you flirting with this hussy." She looked towards Maria.

"She is not a hussy! She is a very nice lady who has just returned the bag we had stolen last week. She's also just told me that the poor young man who handed it in was killed in a road accident on Friday morning."

"He probably deserved it" answered Louise and made her way towards the door. David turned to Maria, shook his head and apologised for her behaviour. Although Louise had really upset him, he didn't show his annoyance.

"I'm sorry about that, Maria. She hasn't been feeling herself lately. Could I pick up this bag when we come back?" David handed the bag over to Maria, and as she took it from his grasp, she deliberately touched his hand and kept her hand on top of his for a few seconds. David looked at her in surprise.

"Thank you for standing up for me just now. It was very gallant of you. I hope you have a very nice day."

David smiled at her. "Louise was out of order, and I was only telling the truth. You are a very nice lady, not to mention gorgeous too. See you later." He turned and ran out of the hotel to catch up with Louise, who by this time was standing on the street waiting for him. Maria smiled, and felt her face redden.

"I'm sorry about that David. I don't know what's wrong with me this morning. I just feel a bit on edge. I shouldn't have said those things," said Louise as soon as David had caught up with her. "Look, there's a lovely bakery just here, can I buy you a doughnut, just as a sort of an apology for my outburst?" David found himself smiling back at her. Louise knew how to manipulate him. She had him wrapped around her little finger.

"Go on then. In fact get me two, and that will be my breakfast."

David didn't know what to make of Louise recently. In fact since the start of their holiday she had been acting very strange. One minute she was so nasty and then the next, so nice. He couldn't make her out. He decided to do what he always did, 'go with the flow'. 'She will come out of these moods whenever she is ready' he thought to himself.

She then appeared with the doughnuts, and they both ate them while standing in the street. Louise was now laughing and joking with David, as she enjoyed her tasty treat. It was as if nothing had happened in the hotel lobby just a few minutes before.

"At least we've got our bag back," she finally remarked.

"Yes, that was a surprise, wasn't it?" answered David as he glanced up at the empty balcony of Juan Marquez.

'There have been a few surprises on this holiday' he thought to himself.

"Now, let's go and see Barcelona!"

Chapter 43

They wanted to see as much of Barcelona as they could, so they wasted no time in scoffing their doughnuts and catching the Barcelona Turistic open air bus. Gaudi's work was of interest to both of them, and as there were so many examples of his architecture throughout the city, they decided to visit three of them.

Firstly they passed La Pedrera, with its irregular shaped balconies, one of his most famous works which had been turned into a museum. Then they visited La Sagrada Familia, a monumental church which he started building in 1882, but according to the commentator on their tour bus, would not be finished for another 20 to 25 years. Finally they went to the Parc Guell, a park full of colourful sculptures, mosaics, and tiled walkways, all created by Gaudi.

It wasn't long before they reached the stop outside the Camp Nou, the home of Barcelona Football Club. This was THE place that David wanted to see most of all, in the city of Barcelona.

He managed to persuade Louise to get off the bus and join him in a tour of the stadium. He loved every minute if it. The highlight of his day was standing in the middle of the home dressing rooms, just thinking of all the famous players who had changed and prepared for a game right there. Players like Maradonna, Cruyff, and Ronaldo. David was happy. He could go home now. He had been to the Camp Nou.

However they still had plenty of places to visit, and their next stop was the Olympic Stadium built for the 1992 Olympic Games. They then took the bus to the Gothic

Quarter, passing by the famous Colon, a memorial to the great explorer Columbus. This was a simple column which stood at the bottom of Las Ramblas. On top was a statue of the great man, hand extended, pointing out to sea. As they neared their destination Louise decided to try and impress David.

"Did you know that Picasso lived and worked in the Gothic Quarter from 1895 until 1904?"

"I'm very impressed. How did you know that?" asked David.

"It says so in this small booklet that we were given when we got on the bus!" David started to laugh and added, "And here's me thinking you were oh so clever, and all the time you are reading out of some book." Louise smiled, took hold of his hand and said, "Come on, I'm taking you to Barcelona Cathedral."

Half an hour later they were walking around the Cathedral. It was awesome. It was so busy and yet so quiet... so many people, and yet so little noise. 'Respect' David thought to himself, 'is such a wonderful thing. I wish there was more respect in today's world!' They left the Cathedral and walked around the square immediately outside, having negotiated the line of beggars hanging around outside the church doors.

It was now raining, and after perusing the bric-a-brac stalls, that filled the square, or junk stalls as David referred to them, they decided to move on. Darkness began to descend on them as they boarded yet another bus which would take them to their last port of call, Montjuic Mountain and The Font Magica. The Magic Fountain, as it is known, is made up of a series of small fountains that shoot water high up into the air amidst shades of red green and yellow coloured lights. This display is accompanied by the music of artists like Whitney Houston, Mozart, and Queen with Freddie Mercury. It is a magical show to witness, especially just as the sun sets on the city. David and Louise were really looking forward to it, but having boarded the bus, the driver informed them that there were no displays on a Monday evening, at this time of the year. They were really gutted, however they quickly changed their itinerary and decided to leave the bus at the stop next to their hotel, and dine in a small Italian restaurant just across the road. David ordered spaghetti carbonara, and Louise settled for lasagne along with plenty of French bread. Since it was their final night, they washed it all down with a bottle of their favourite wine, Chateau Neuf Du Pape. It was an excellent meal, and all they had to do now, was to walk across the road to their hotel, which was an added bonus.

It was still raining, and Barcelona seemed very quiet and peaceful as they entered the hotel and David approached the desk to collect the room key. He was disappointed that Maria had finished her shift, as he had wanted to apologise once again for that morning's escapade. She was also keeping his returned luggage bag for him, but that would have to wait now.

'I'll see her tomorrow' he thought to himself.

Up in the room, Louise suddenly seemed a little on edge and immediately changed into her pyjamas. "I'm really tired, I'm going to bed. What are you going to do David?"

"Well, it's only ten o'clock, so I'm going to sit on the balcony and have a couple of drinks. You get a good night's sleep, we have a long day tomorrow. Goodnight." At that time he didn't realise how prophetic those words would turnout to be. It would be a very long day.

He poured himself a vodka and diet coke and sat out on the balcony. Although it was raining, it certainly wasn't cold. It was a warm evening, and there was hardly a sound coming from the streets below. It was very, very quiet, eerily so. All was calm as he looked across to the empty balcony of Juan Marquez, and thought about the first time he had met him. It seemed more than eight days ago.

He sipped his drink and thought to himself, 'What a strange holiday this has been .We've had our bag stolen in Barcelona, and then got it back one week later! The only witness to the incident said that my wife handed the bag to the thief! The bag had been returned by someone who was now dead! The case has been handled by the Assistant Chief of Police! I've been knocked down by a car in Naples, and thought my wife had pushed me in front of it! And now I'm sitting here all alone in the centre of Barcelona and there's not a sound to be heard! At least it's a peaceful end to the holiday.'

What David didn't know was that this in fact was the calm before the storm!

Chapter 44

It was Tuesday, the last day of their holiday, and the plan was to have a late breakfast and then a walkabout around the district surrounding their hotel. They managed to accomplish part of the plan, the late breakfast part, but they had to abandon their idea of a stroll around the nearby streets, as it had started raining again. So they returned to their room, finished packing, and then chilled out on the balcony for an hour or two, just reading their books.

At one o'clock David left Louise reading and went down to reception to collect his stolen, but now returned, luggage bag. He knew that Maria, who was keeping the bag for him, started her shift at that time.

"Good afternoon Maria, we are going home tonight, so what time do we have to check-out of our rooms?"

"One o'clock David, but you don't have to rush."

"Do you have a room where we can put our cases?"

"Yes, just here," and she pointed to a door to her right hand side. "They will be safe in there. I will give you a ticket, and even if I'm not here, just show it at reception and someone will get your cases for you. The key is always here."

"That's great Maria. I'll just go and get our cases, and if you give me my 'stolen' bag I will put it in there as well. See you soon." Ten minutes later David was back at the reception desk. After watching the bellboy put their cases into the luggage room, and getting his ticket from Maria, David and Louise went for lunch. As it was raining they decided to go to the Café Magic, just at the end of the street. They wouldn't be venturing far today.

After a quick lunch they ran back across the road to their hotel, as it had started to rain even heavier. David settled into one of the comfy seats which adorned the foyer and started to read his James Patterson novel. Louise took a seat just next to him and within a minute was totally engrossed in her magazine. The time just flew by, and before they knew it, it was five o'clock. David put his book down, rubbed his eyes, and stretched his arms skywards.

"We'll go for the quarter past seven train to the airport, which should get us there about twenty to eight. Does that sound alright to you?" asked David.

"What time do we have to check in?" asked Louise.

"Quarter past eight."

"Agreed," answered Louise, and then asked, "Would you like a doughnut?" She was feeling a bit peckish again. She asked David to watch her bag, then got up and walked out of the hotel, heading towards the bakery just a few doors down the street, all the while being ogled by the bell-boy and the sleazy looking concierge. As she reached the end of the huge hotel window and disappeared out of his view, a terrible feeling arose within David's being- a feeling that he was never going to see her again. He shook his head, gave himself a reprimand -'don't be so silly'- and continued to read his book. Ten minutes later Louise still hadn't returned but David was trying not to worry. He decided that the bakery must be busy. He sat there all alone, looking out through the large hotel window, watching, hoping, and waiting for her to re-appear.

Just then a beautiful black Jaguar X- type Sovereign with dark tinted windows gracefully glided to a halt outside of the hotel. The driver got out of the car and proceeded to open the back door for his passenger. Out came a gentleman wearing black trousers, shining black shoes, a crisp white shirt and a maroon coloured blazer draped over his shoulders. He was about five feet eight inches in height, and had perfectly coiffeured grey/black hair. This was clearly a very important person as far as this hotel was concerned, because as soon as he got out of the car, every employee in reception started brushing down their trousers or skirts, tucked their shirts in properly, and straightened their ties........ even the sleazy concierge. As the man walked towards the hotel doors, the driver got back into the gently purring Jaguar and drove smoothly down the street obviously looking for a parking space. David was enjoying watching this entertaining scenario.

The man came through the doors to be welcomed by a chorus of 'Good evening Senor Martinez." David likened it to a class of school children greeting their teacher. He smiled. The gentleman acknowledged their welcome, walked behind the desk and started talking to the staff who were working the desk that evening. After about ten minutes Senor Martinez came out from behind reception and walked straight over to David. "Good evening sir, are you enjoying your stay at the hotel?"

"Yes thanks, it's been lovely." David stood up and introduced himself. "David Telfer, pleased to meet you. Do you work here?" He held out his hand, which the man then shook.

"Carlos Angel Martinez, I own the hotel, it's a pleasure to meet you. Are you here on your own?"

"No, I'm here with my wife. We go home tonight but we've loved your hotel and thoroughly enjoyed our holiday. We hope to come back some day."

"Well I'm glad to hear that. I hope you have a safe journey home." Carlos turned around and walked over towards the door, at the same time signalling to reception to phone for his car. Two minutes later it arrived at the front door. He said goodbye to all of his staff and then looked over towards David and shouted "I hope you find your wife!" He then turned and walked away.

David watched the car slowly drive away and thought to himself ---'what a strange thing to say.'

Chapter 45

It was half past five and David was getting a bit worried now. He placed his book down on the chair, lifted Louise's bag and decided to go and find her. He felt rather awkward as he crossed the foyer carrying a ladies handbag, so he tried to hide it as he walked out of the revolving door. He was now standing outside the bakery, looking in through the window. Louise was nowhere to be seen. He turned around, looked left and then right, up and down the street. No Louise. He went into the bakery and asked the assistant if a blonde lady had been in the shop buying doughnuts, within the last half hour. The assistant could only speak broken English, but she gave David a clear enough answer.

"No blonde lady. No donuts from una hora."

"Are you sure of that?" asked David. The lady pointed to the clock and answered,

"Si. Una hora,.. donuts fini. No more donuts. From cuatro hora, no senoritas in aqui.... here. Only tres hombres." She held up three fingers.

David thanked the lady, left the shop, walked down to the end of the street and turned right towards the Sants Railway station, hoping that she had decided to go for a stroll, or maybe to check the train timetable. He didn't really believe this, as she had a terrible sense of direction and never ventured off on her own when they were in a strange town or city. The station was really busy at that time of night, but he had a good look around anyway, but to no avail. He looked up at the station clock to see that the time was already approaching ten past six. 'That's been over an hour she's been gone' he thought. 'She might have returned to the hotel by now.' David started running back towards the hotel, still clutching Louise's handbag, but he no longer felt awkward. He had more important things to worry about.

He slowed down when he reached the baker's shop and looked in the window again. The shop was empty. In fact they were just closing up for the day. He then ran into the hotel and immediately approached Maria and asked her if she had seen Louise.

"Yes" she replied.

David felt a tremendous sense of relief flow through his whole body.

"Where is she?"

"I don't know where she is now, but I saw her just over an hour ago, going out of the front doors."

"Sorry Maria, but I meant within the last hour. Have you seen her since then?"

"No, I'm sorry David."

David stood motionless in the middle of the foyer. He didn't know what to do next.

'Why is this happening to me?' he asked himself.

And then it hit him!

Her mobile phone! Louise never ventured anywhere without her mobile.

'Why didn't I think of this before?' he thought, as he hurriedly tried to pull his cell phone from his jeans pocket.

'All I have to do is call Louise, find out where she is, and then give her directions on how to get back to the hotel. If she can't follow my directions, I'll just go and get her!'

Everything was so clear in his mind now. It was all so simple. He threw Louise's bag down on to the nearest chair, and pressed number one on his mobile, Louise's speed dial number. A few seconds passed before the call actually connected and started to ring out. He looked up at the hotel clock to see that it was half past six....plenty of time to get Louise back to the hotel and then over to the station to catch the 7-15 train as planned. David was much calmer now and chastised himself for getting so worked up.

The seconds passed by and still no answer.

David walked around the foyer with his mobile pressed against his right ear, willing Louise to answer.

'Please answer Louise, Please!' he mumbled to himself, as he headed over to the seat where Louise's bag lay. He was becoming anxious again.

And then his whole world collapsed around him!

He could faintly hear the Kylie Minogue song 'Can't get you out of my head'.....Louise's ring tone. He knew in an instant that she wouldn't answer. She didn't have her phone.

She had left it in her bag!

David turned and ran back out onto the street. He returned to the bakery to ask the assistant if she was positive that she hadn't seen Louise, but the shop was now closed. He turned and started to run back to the hotel. He stopped and looked in through the huge hotel window hoping to see her sitting on the chair she had been sitting on earlier, but there was no sign of her. The anxiety was beginning to overwhelm him now. He started running in the opposite direction towards the main street at the other end of the hotel. It was very busy. He mingled with the throngs of people walking along the crowded pavement, hoping to catch a glimpse of Louise, perhaps window shopping. But he knew she didn't like shopping so he didn't hold out much hope. He gave up about twenty minutes later and started running back to the Sants Hotel once again. He didn't know what time it was, but he knew it must be close to 7-15, the time they had decided to leave for the airport.

Back at the hotel he frantically pushed his way through the revolving doors, and rushed up to the reception desk. It was very crowded with people checking in, but Maria seeing that he was looking so distressed, excused herself from her client, and asked one of her colleagues to take over. David's hair was dishevelled, his shirt was hanging out, he was soaking with sweat, and he was out of breath. He looked a mess.

"David, what's wrong with you?"

"Maria, I need your help! It's seven o'clock and we are supposed to be leaving at quarter past seven."

"So what do you want me to do David?"

"Don't you understand Maria? Louise is missing. I can't find my wife!"

Chapter 46

Carlos hadn't heard from Assistant Chief Ramirez since Sunday night and he was getting a tad anxious. Ramirez, the Fixer, had told him then, that he would fix his blackmailing problem.

"Don't worry" he had said, "I'll fix it."

'It's alright him saying that, but it's not him who is about to run for Mayor' he thought to himself, as he sipped his glass of malt whisky. 'I can't bear having this hanging over my head!' He hadn't received any calls from Juan Marquez either, and he was beginning to think he had changed his mind and gone directly to the newspapers to sell his photos.

He was sitting in silence, in the living room of his home in Sitges. The house was so quiet because every Tuesday he gave all his housing staff the day off. This was his personal space where he came when he needed time to think, or when he had a problem to solve. He had also used it in the past for some extra marital fun and games. His wife didn't even know this house existed.

He closed his eyes and laid his head down on the back of the leather sofa. Just as he was falling asleep, he was startled by a distant bleeping sound. It took a few moments for him to realise that it was the sound of his telephone. He jumped up, shook off his sleep and grabbed the phone. It was Gilberto Ramirez.

"About time too, Gilberto, I've been waiting for you to call. What's happening?"

"It's fixed Carlos. I spoke to Juan Marquez on Saturday night and I managed to persuade him that it would not be in his best interest to continue with his present demands, with regards to you. I told him that I knew all about his criminal activities, but I would turn a blind eye if he did what I told him."

"And what did he say to that?"

"He agreed."

"And that was it. It was as simple as that? And what about the photographs, did you get them?" asked Carlos.

"It was that simple. As for the photos, he didn't have them in the house, but I will get them. And I can assure you, you won't have any more problems with Juan Marquez."

"So he doesn't want any money now?"

"Not one euro. Have a nice evening Carlos. Buenas Noches."

'All's well that ends well' thought Carlos as he put the phone back in its cradle, finished his whisky, lay down on the sofa and fell into a deep, stress-free, relaxing sleep.

Chapter 47

"Try to calm down David" said Maria as she pushed the open palms of her hands in a downward motion towards the floor. "When and where did you last see your wife?"

"Five o'clock, when she left here to go to the bakery two doors down. She was only going for a doughnut! She should have been back ages ago. That's when you saw her going out of that door."

He pointed towards the revolving doors.

"So, I take it you have checked the bakery. Where else have you looked?" enquired Maria.

David thought for a moment and then answered, "I checked up and down the street outside, then ran over to the train station and had a look around, inside and out. After that I came back and looked in the bakery and the hotel again. Then I walked up and down the busy street around the corner, at the other side of the hotel. And now I'm back here and still no Louise."

"Okay, let's not panic" said Maria. "Wait there, I'll be back in a second." Maria then went over to explain the situation to her boss, and to ask him for permission to help David look for his wife. He agreed immediately, and Maria rejoined David who was nervously pacing up and down the foyer, rubbing the front of his forehead with his right hand.

"Maria, it's ten past seven, Louise and I should be standing on the platform waiting for our train."

"You still have plenty of time to get to the airport" said Maria. "Have you looked in the bar or restaurant on the third floor? What about the Café Magic at the end of the road?"

"No, I haven't."

"Okay. I have some time off to help you find Louise, so we'll split up and you can go up to the third floor and have a look there, while I have another look around outside, before I check the Café Magic. If we can't find her I will call the police for you when we meet back here. Are you happy with that?"

"That's Fine. Thank you so much Maria."

They then parted company and carried out their respective searches, Maria asking questions in and around the café, and David doing exactly the same in the hotel bar. But it was all to no avail. Louise seemed to have vanished off the face of the earth. It was quarter to eight when David and Maria met up again in the hotel foyer. David was distraught.

"Do you want me to call the police now?" Maria asked David who was now sitting on the sofa he had been sitting on earlier, with his head in his hands. He couldn't even speak now, to answer Maria, so he just nodded his head.

Maria called the police from reception and then rejoined David.

"Someone will be here from the Mossos d'Esquadra shortly. Now do you want a brandy or a whisky, just to calm you down a little?" David didn't really want a drink but thought that it might indeed calm his nerves.

"Yes please Maria, I think that might be a good idea. Can I have a malt whisky, please? In fact make it a double." He took some money out of his pocket to pay for the drink, but Maria wouldn't hear of it, and told him it was 'on the house'.

Two hour later, quarter to ten, and the police had still not arrived. Maria had already phoned again and they had promised to be there as quick as possible. David had been in and out of the hotel one hundred times hoping to catch a glimpse of Louise, but now he was back sitting on his sofa next to Maria. He was on his third malt whisky.

"What the fuck is keeping them Maria. My bag was stolen and they were here in five minutes. My wife disappears and it takes them hours to get here. What kind of fucking police force is this?" He paused for a moment, and then apologised to Maria for swearing.

"It's okay David, I know how upset you are."

"How can you know how upset I am?" David snapped. "You've never lost your wife like this, have you?" You don't know how it feels!" As soon as David had said it, he wished he hadn't.

"I'm sorry Maria, I shouldn't have said that, especially after all the help you have given me."

"Apology accepted, but I do know how you feel. I lost my younger brother 10 years ago. I was 29 years old and my brother was only sixteen."

"I'm so sorry to hear that, Maria. What happened?"

"He was young and naïve, and unfortunately he got caught up with the wrong type of people. He was in a street gang and got mixed up with drugs. He delivered the drugs for the gang leaders and then took the money back to them. However on one occasion he decided he was due some extra cash for himself. So he finished his drug run, but instead of taking the money back to his masters, he disappeared for a few weeks. My mother and I didn't know what had happened to him, and we frantically searched the city, looking for him. Just like you did, when you realised Louise was missing."

"And did you find him?"

"No, but he turned up out of the blue, six weeks later, as if nothing had happened. We were ecstatic, but at the same time angry, because he could have let us know he was safe, with just one phone call."

"And was everything settled with the drug dealers?"

"Yes, it was settled alright. The very next night after he had returned, they broke into our house and shot him dead as he lay in his bed. He had tried to reach the gun that he always kept hidden under his mattress, but he never made it in time. I still have that gun, a Glock 17, and I now keep it hidden under my mattress. It helps me get to sleep at night. I will never forget that terrible evening." She paused for a moment then added, "so, you see David, I do know how you feel."

"I'm so sorry Maria. You must think I'm one ignorant and selfish bastard! I didn't realise" said David trying to redeem the situation.

"It's okay, as I have said already, I know how you must be feeling."

David looked at Maria and then leaned forward and hugged her. She in turn wrapped her arms around him, and they both just sat there with tears in their eyes, joined together in grief. It seemed like an eternity, but their embrace only lasted for several seconds before both of them leaned back on the sofa and lost themselves in their own thoughts.

They had been sitting there in complete silence for a full ten minutes, before David suddenly straightened up in his seat. "Maria I've just thought of something. I'll be back in five minutes." He got up and walked across the foyer with a real purpose in his step. He shouted back to Maria.

"Juan Marquez! I forgot about Juan Marquez. He is always on his balcony. He might have seen her. I'm going across to ask him."

He was nearly out of the door when Maria called him. "David, come back!" He came back through the revolving doors in the same revolution and stood just inside the door.

"What is it?"

"There's no point going over there David."

"What do you mean Maria, there's no point in going over there! He is always on that balcony. He knows what Louise looks like. He might have seen her!"

"David, Juan Marquez was killed on Saturday night."

Chapter 48

The two young policemen arrived at exactly quarter past ten, ironic really, because that was the departure time of Louise and David's flight leaving Barcelona. They looked hardly out of their teens. Maria approached them as soon as they entered the hotel. She had finished work for the night, but was waiting in case the police wanted to ask her anything, as it was she who had actually reported Louise missing. She spoke to them in Spanish for a few minutes and then introduced David to them. "This is David Telfer, the gentleman whose wife is missing." The taller of the two then started asking David questions, while the other one took down some notes.

"Have you been drinking, Mr Telfer?"

"Yes, Maria suggested a drink to calm my nerves! Why? What are you inferring?"

"I'm not inferring anything sir. I just thought I could smell drink off your breath. How many have you had?"

"I've had three whiskies. Why? What has this got to do with the fact that my wife is missing?"

"Did your wife have some drinks with you before she left?"

"No. I've only had a couple of drinks to calm me down, and that's after Louise disappeared!"

"When did you last see your wife, sir?

"Five o'clock."

"And where was that?"

"She was walking along the pavement right in front of that big window." He then pointed over to the large hotel window.

"Where was she going?"

"She was going to get something to eat from the bakery, two doors down."

"Is that the last time you saw her?"

"Yes. We were supposed to be catching the 7-15 train to take us to the airport, but she never came back. Our flight was leaving at 10-15. As you can see, we've missed it."

"Are you here on holiday?"

"Yes, we were on a cruise and we stayed here for one night before, and then two nights after."

"Are you here with anyone else... with other friends, perhaps?"

"No. There's just the two of us."

"You didn't have an argument with your wife, did you sir?"

"NO I DIDN'T." David was shouting now. "She felt a bit peckish so she went to get a doughnut, that's all. No arguments. At first I thought she might have got lost, but I know that's not the case."

"How do you know sir? Let me tell you something. It's very easy to get lost in Barcelona."

"She is not lost." David quickly answered.

"You may think that sir, but you only have to take one wrong turn. It's such a big city."

"I don't think she is lost."

"I have known people who have been lost in Barcelona for a full day," the officer added.

"She isn't lost!"

"I have a friend who has lived here for two years and he still gets lost."

David was getting agitated. He didn't like the officer's tone when he asked him if he had been drinking, and all this talk of being 'lost' was irritating him. He thought they should be out searching for her, rather wasting all this time. He couldn't take any more.

He exploded.

"She is not fucking lost. How the fuck can you get lost going to the shop just next door? She was only going for doughnuts. Believe me, something has happened to her."

"Calm down, sir. We are only trying to help." The young officer gave David a few moments to compose himself before he asked his next question.

"Do you have any recent photographs of your wife?"

"I'm sorry officer, but I'm just so worried about her. We should be sitting on a plane, flying home right now." He paused for a second. "Yes I have plenty of photos in my mobile phone."

He started to scroll down all the pictures of Louise while the policeman looked over his shoulder.

"Can I take your phone to the station and I will scan some of the best photos, and then we will start looking for your wife. In the meantime, would you like to go with Officer Fernandez and he will drive around the local area, and you can lookout for her. Okay?"

"Yes, I would. Thank you."

David turned to Maria who had just re-appeared at his side and thanked her for all her help. "I've booked the same room for you for tonight. Here is your key. We can sort all the details out in the morning. I start at eight" said Maria.

"Oh Maria, I never even thought about where I was staying tonight. I've got too much on my mind. Thank you very much."

"No problem. I hope you find your wife when you are out searching with Officer Fernandez. If not, try and get a good night's sleep when you return. I will see you in the morning. Buenas Noches."

"Thanks again Maria, but I don't think sleep will come easy tonight." He then followed the young officer out of the hotel and into the waiting car.

Chapter 49

David was right. Sleep didn't come easy that night. In fact he hadn't slept a wink. He had driven around Barcelona for three hours with Officer Fernandez, but with no luck. He had finally returned to his room at two o'clock in the morning, but rather than go to bed, he had sat on the balcony all night, just looking out, hoping that Louise would magically appear on the streets below. It was now 8-30 a.m., and he was standing in a hot shower wondering what he was going to do in the day ahead. A thousand different thoughts ran through his mind....the first night he had met Louise, the holidays they had taken together, the day they had moved into their new house, their wedding day. So many happy memories.....and now he couldn't find her. Where was she? The tears streamed down his cheeks. He felt so alone. He stood in that shower for a full half hour before deciding to get dried and dressed. However he didn't have any clean clothes, as his cases were still in the luggage room downstairs, so he decided to go down and take the cases back up to the room and then start the day with fresh clothes.

'I'll have to get myself organised today, and book this room for a couple of more nights. Then I'll have to phone my boss and let him know what's happening. I'll have to be strong today and every other day until I find Louise.'

Those were the thoughts in David's mind as he walked downstairs to collect his cases. He preferred to walk rather than take the lift, so that he could clear his head. He also thought that the lifts would be busy at that time, and he didn't really want to have to make polite conversation with some stranger in a lift. But he couldn't wait to get to reception to find out if there had been any developments. He opened the door which led into the foyer and the first person he noticed was Assistant Chief Ramirez.

"Good morning Senor Telfer, we meet again. I'm sorry it's always been in unhappy circumstances. How are you feeling this morning? How did you sleep?"

"Not too good. In fact, I never slept at all. Have you any news for me?"

"Well, I'm sorry that I can't tell you that we've found your wife, but we are making some progress already. We have set up a small office in the corner of the foyer over there, and we have already started taking statements from hotel staff and guests."

"What can I do to help?" asked David.

"Firstly, you can answer a few questions. Has your wife ever done anything like this before? Just gone off on her own, without telling you?"

"Not recently."

"What do you mean, not recently?"

"Some years ago, my wife suffered from depression, and when she felt stressed she sometimes just disappeared for a few days. She didn't do it very often."

"Do you think she has been feeling stressed recently. For example, could the incident when your bag was stolen have triggered anything off? Could that have upset her enough to walk away like this?"

"It might have. To be honest, I have been worried about her during our holiday. She has been acting a bit strange lately."

"In what way?"

"Well, all through our holiday, in Naples, Mdina, and Cannes, Louise felt she was being followed. She said that someone was stalking her. Also, one minute she would be nice to me, and then the next, she would be cruel. I didn't know what to make of her at times. At one point in Naples, I even thought she had tried to kill me"

"What do you mean? What happened?"

"I was waiting to cross the road in Naples, and I was pushed in front of a car. The car hardly touched me."

"And you thought your wife did it?"

"Louise was standing directly behind me, so I blamed her to start with, but there were so many people waiting to cross the road that anyone could have bumped into me and knocked me in front of that car."

"So you are now sure that it wasn't her who pushed you?"

"Well, I'm satisfied that it wasn't Louise. And even if it was, it was accidental."

"Fine, I have one final question. In the past, when she did go off somewhere, did she usually return of her own accord?"

"Yes, she did."

"You've been very helpful Mr Telfer. Now, I would like you to go with one of my officers and retrace your steps, not only from yesterday, but also from the previous day, when I believe you took a tour of the city. Hopefully, if she is wandering around Barcelona in some sort of distressed state, she will go back to some place she has already visited, like Barcelona Cathedral for example. Good luck, I will see you when you return."

David took his cases back up to the room, changed into fresh clothes, and then left the hotel on the first day of his search for Louise, little realising that this case was soon going to go down a road that he could never have expected.

Chapter 50

David returned to the hotel six hours later, at four o'clock in the afternoon. It had been another unsuccessful foray into the streets of Barcelona, but he would try again by himself after he had sorted out his room for the next week, had some dinner, and contacted his boss at work. First of all he went to reception, and was pleased to see that Maria was working. She was so easy to talk to, and so helpful.

"Thanks Maria, for sorting out my room last night. I would like to book it for another week please, if possible." Just at that, Carlos Martinez appeared from the back office. "Buenas diaz Senor Telfer, I'm sorry to hear about your wife. I felt so guilty this morning when I heard about your wife's disappearance. I couldn't help thinking about the last words I said to you last night. 'I hope you find your wife.' I was only trying to make a joke, and then she actually disappears. I'm so sorry!"

"It's okay Senor Martinez, it's not your fault, you weren't to know that this was going to happen" said a visibly shaken David.

"Please call me Carlos. And as for the room, you can stay here as long as you need to, free of charge. It's the least I can do. I've also instructed Maria to help you in any way she can, and let's hope we can find your wife." He then walked away to his waiting car.

"Maria, I forgot to take my 'stolen' bag up to my room this morning, I left it in the luggage room. My mind is so mixed up, could I have it now, please. And there's something else that I would like to ask you, if you can give me five minutes of your time" asked David. Maria shouted for one of her colleagues to cover for her, then duly went and retrieved David's bag from the luggage room, and then joined him on one of the foyer sofas.

"What do you know about Juan Marquez's death?"

"Just that it was a terrible accident. He fell from his balcony on Saturday night."

"Did anyone see it happen?"

"No, there were no witnesses. A passer by found his body lying in the street. Seemingly he was dead as soon as he hit the ground."

"I see. It's just that I find all of this very strange. We have our bag stolen, and now the only two people I know that are connected in any way to the theft, have both been killed by accident...Emilio Torres and Juan Marquez. And now my wife has mysteriously disappeared!"

"That IS very strange. I hadn't thought of that" said Maria. "I will ask Alfonso if he can tell me anything about his death when he comes back to work. He knew Juan Marquez."

"Thanks. That might be really helpful. It also means that there are only two people left who were directly involved with the theft... myself and Assistant Chief Ramirez, who is now in charge of my wife's disappearance. I can't help thinking that I may be next on that list, and that something bad is going to happen to me!"

David then rose and thanked Maria for her time, and as he did, he unzipped his 'stolen' bag to check if his shoes were still there, as they would be much more comfortable for walking around the city later on. He had forgotten all about them being in the bag. As he finally pulled them out from the bottom, he noticed a folded A4 piece of paper.

"There's a note in here Maria" said David as he pulled it out. He opened it as Maria walked round behind him to see what was written on it. In black felt tip pen it read:

We have you wife. If you want to see her again you will have to pay us one million euros.

Chapter 51

Half an hour later and Sergeant Villa was in the hotel, introducing himself to David.

"Buenas diaz, Senor Telfer. My name is Sergeant Villa and this is Officer Fernandez, who I believe you have already met. I'm sorry, but Assistant Chief Ramirez sends his apologies, he couldn't come. I'm afraid his wife died suddenly last night."

"But that can't be right. He interviewed me this morning."

"That's correct sir. Assistant Chief Ramirez was attending a Police Conference in Zaragoza, all day Tuesday. He stayed over, got up at six o'clock this morning and drove the three hours back to Barcelona...straight to this hotel really. For some unknown reason the hospital failed to contact him until after he spoke to you. So, in the meantime he has put me in charge of this investigation."

David took an immediate dislike to the forty year old well built, balding sergeant, who seemed to have no neck. He looked like a mini Mike Tyson. But it wasn't his looks that David didn't like. It was the fact that he seemed very abrupt.

"I believe you found a note in the bag that has been returned. Let me see it."

David handed the note to the sergeant who was now wearing white latex gloves. "Has anyone else handled this note?"

"No"

"I've been informed that your bag was returned to this hotel last Wednesday, so why haven't you checked it before now?" David didn't like the cheeky manner in which the sergeant was asking his questions.

"I didn't return to this hotel until Sunday night. My wife and I were on a cruise."

"I repeat. Why has it taken you so long to check it?"

"Well, I only got it back on Monday."

"If I had my bag stolen, and then returned, I would check it immediately" Officer Villa replied cheekily.

"Look, I checked most of it. I just didn't take everything out until half an hour ago. It was only then that I noticed the note, right at the bottom of the bag."

"Did anyone witness you taking the note from the bag?"

"I did" answered Maria. "Why do you ask?"

"No particular reason" he replied as he turned towards Maria and added, "I take it that you are Maria?"

"That's right, I was with him when he opened the bag."

"That's fine Maria." He then turned and faced David again.

"Mr Telfer, can you clear something up for me. When your wife disappeared yesterday, had you been drinking?"

"No I had not! Why do you ask that?"

"Well the officer who interviewed you last night wrote in his report that you had been drinking whisky. Is he telling lies?"

"No he isn't. But that was after my wife disappeared, just to steady my nerves. In fact it was Maria who suggested it."

Sergeant Villa pondered for a moment, and then continued.

"Is it true that you had an argument with your wife in this hotel reception area on Monday morning?"

"Who told you that?"

"Never mind sir, please answer the question."

"No, it wasn't an argument. She just wasn't happy with me because I left her in the room by herself. She came down and shouted some things at me. That's all. It was no big deal."

"I've also been told that your wife thought she was being stalked while on the cruise. Did you feel at any time, that someone was following you?"

"Actually, there were moments when I thought we were being watched. It was a funny feeling."

Sergeant Villa then stopped his interrogation just as suddenly as he had started, and placed the note into a clear plastic bag, and sealed it.

"I will get this to the lab to be checked for finger-prints, and as soon as we get the results I will let you know. Obviously, this changes everything, as far as our line of investigation goes" he said as he held up the poly bag. "If anyone tries to contact you, let me know immediately. I will be in touch. Adios."

"Don't worry I will. Adios" replied David as he watched him walk over to the hotel doors. He was glad to see the back of him, quite literally, the cheeky bastard. But he wasn't prepared for Sergeant Villa's parting shot as he turned round to face David.

"One thing I forgot to mention, Mr Telfer. Make sure you don't leave Barcelona!"

Chapter 52

David left Maria, who returned to her desk, while he went up to his room to change his shoes, and to phone his workplace to explain his predicament. His boss was very sympathetic towards him, and told him to take as much time off as he needed, in order to find his wife.

"If I can help in any way at all, just call me. Your wages will be put into the bank just as normal this Friday. Good luck, and phone me if you have any news." David felt better when he heard his boss's words, because in years gone by, he had taken a lot of time off to look after Louise, and he didn't want his boss to think he was taking him for granted.

Now that he had informed his work and sorted out his room for the foreseeable future, he re-focused his mind on his current problem, his wife's alleged kidnapping. He was still stunned with Villa's orders 'not to leave Barcelona', and couldn't believe that, deep down, Villa obviously had it in his mind, that he had something to do with Louise's disappearance. He had also noticed that Villa had already taken away the small office set up in the corner of the hotel foyer, by Assistant Chief Ramirez. There was now no police presence in the hotel. Villa really wanted to stamp his authority on this case, and it looked as if he thought David was involved. With this in mind, David decided that he would keep looking for Louise on his own, but he would need a little help from Maria.

She was working in reception as usual when David approached her.

"Maria, could you take some of the photographs of Louise that I have in my mobile phone, and print them off for me? Can you do that?"

"Yes, I can do that, David. What do you plan to do with them?"

"I'm going to walk the streets of Barcelona showing the pictures to anyone I meet, in the hope that someone recognises her. I'm also going to stick them up at all the main tourist haunts. I'll put my mobile number on there as well, so that they can contact me. What do you think?"

"I think that's better than sitting about the hotel doing nothing, because I don't think that Officer Villa is going to be much help to you. In fact, I think that he has the impression that you are involved somehow. When you went up to your room, he came back in and asked me some questions about you."

"What kind of questions?"

"Had I seen you drinking a lot of alcohol? Did I see you arguing with your wife, apart from that Monday morning? Did I think you and Louise had a good relationship? Did I see you sitting in the foyer all of the time, the night Louise disappeared?

"And what did you say?"

"I said that I didn't know the two of you well enough, to comment on your relationship, but that I hadn't seen you arguing, and that everything looked okay."

"And what about the last question?"

"I told the truth. I didn't see you all of the time, I was working. I did see you sitting there when Senor Martinez came in and spoke to you, but after that I didn't really notice you, until you asked me about Louise, some time later. I was too busy."

"Maria, I don't believe this, but I think he is trying to build a case against me. Why did he ask if any one witnessed me pulling out that kidnap note? Why did he ask you about my relationship with Louise? I don't know what he's up to, but I've a funny feeling I'm going to find out sooner rather than later."

"I think you're right, David. Do you know the best thing you can do to get him off your back."

"What's that?"

"Find Louise!"

Chapter 53

It was now eight o'clock and Maria had finished copying the photos of Louise, just as Alfonso came in through the door to start his shift. He took his jacket off as he walked behind the desk, into the back office. When he reappeared David could see Maria talking to him, and that the man had become very animated. However after a few minutes chat, he seemed to have calmed down, and it was then that he started to walk over to David, who was sitting on one of the sofas.

"Buenas noches Mr Telfer. My name is Alfonso, I believe you want to know about Juan Marquez."

"Yes. You see, Juan Marquez was a witness to our bag theft, which I actually spoke to him about, before we went on our cruise. And now two people who I know were connected with the theft are dead-Juan Marquez and Emilio Torres. Not only that, my wife is now missing. I was wondering if it was somehow all connected. Can you help me, please? I'm desperate to find my wife!"

Alfonso had already noticed that David did indeed look like a desperate man!

"What I am about to tell you, you can never repeat Mr Telfer, or I will get into big trouble and lose my job. Do you promise not to tell anyone?"

"I promise" David replied in the most sincere voice he could muster.

Alfonso then started to tell his story.

"I had a little business going with Juan Marquez. I selected people in this hotel, who I thought were having illicit affairs, and pointed them out to Juan. He took pictures of them, and then sold them the photographs, so that they didn't fall into the wrong hands."

"Sold them? You mean blackmailed them!"

"You can call it what you like, but last week Juan took some photos of someone who is a public figure in Barcelona. That's all he would tell me. He didn't pick him or her... Juan just struck it lucky. He told me that this person would pay a lot of money for the photos, and that I would get a bigger payout than normal. Then he has an accident and dies, that's very strange, don't you think?"

"Yes, very. Do you think he was murdered?"

"I think he was, but I can't prove it. But I think it does show that his death has nothing to do with your bag theft, or your wife's disappearance. Don't you agree?"

"I do, and thank you for divulging that information. I can see how it could get you into trouble!"

"That's alright, Maria is a good friend. I hope you find your wife" said Alfonso as he turned and walked back to his post.

David then went to reception and Maria handed him the photos that she had copied.

"Thanks Maria. Now wish me luck."

"Good luck, David. Be careful out there, Barcelona can be a very dangerous place, especially after dark."

David just smiled and headed out onto the streets of Barcelona.

Chapter 54

David returned to the hotel at two o'clock in the morning, feeling tired, dirty and disconsolate. He had walked for miles and hadn't come up with anything. He had asked hundreds of people if they had seen Louise, but no one recognised her. He had put the thirty four photos he had taken with him, up at various places around the city. Outside of La Padrera. La Sagrada Familia, in and around La Placa De Catalunya, and up and down Las Ramblas. 'Tomorrow he would get more photos from Maria, and stick them up on more spots throughout the city.' That was what was in his mind as he tried to get to sleep.

That was the same scenario for the next three days and nights. Trudging around the streets, grabbing something to eat, puting posters up anywhere he could, showing people photos of Louise, and then returning to the hotel in the early hours. He didn't receive any phone calls regarding his posters, nor did he receive any message from the supposed kidnappers. He didn't know what to do next.

His mind was made up for him at seven o'clock that Sunday morning when he heard someone banging on his hotel room door. His first thought was that it might be Louise in a panic, desperate to reach the safety of her hotel room. He rushed over to the room door, but then he heard a man's voice shouting for him to open up. David stopped in his tracks. "Who is it?"

"It's the police. Open up."

David felt relieved, but also confused. Maybe they had found Louise, but then why all the banging and shouting? He walked over and started to unlock the door, but as soon as he turned the key, the two policemen pushed the door back, and David flew back across the room onto the floor. He rose to his feet and started shouting at the police.

"What the fuck is this all about? There's no need to be so rough!"

One of the officers walked over to him, drew his baton and whacked David on the back of his legs. David screamed. The pain was intense. He wasn't even wearing any trousers to give him at least some protection.

"Get ready, you are coming with us. Sergeant Villa wants to speak to you."

"Why? What am I supposed to have done?" The other officer took his turn at hitting David with his baton, and he let out another shriek. He didn't say another word. He had heard stories about police brutality in Spain, and now he was experiencing it for himself. When he had put his clothes on, both the officers grabbed a wrist each and marched him down to reception, and out into the waiting police car.

David was in a daze. He had come on holiday for ten days, his wife was missing and now he was going to find himself in a Spanish jail. How could this be happening to him?

And to make matters worse, it seemed that the Officer in charge had it in for him.

Chapter 55

David was escorted into the police station by the two officers still holding his wrists. He was taken along a corridor, and then hurled into a small dingy room, in which there stood a table and three chairs, one on one side of the table and two on the other. They closed the door behind him and walked away.

One hour later Officer Villa entered the room accompanied by another officer whom David hadn't seen before. They had deliberately kept him waiting for the hour, it was part of their plan. Make him sweat! They both circled the table and then sat down directly across from him. Villa started speaking in a low gentle voice.

"Do you know why you are here?"

"All I was told was that you wanted to speak to me. I am at a loss as to why I have been treated so badly this morning! I thought that the officers that you sent were going to give me some good news about my wife, but instead they beat me with their batons and dragged me down here. What the fuck is going on?"

Villa struck him across the face with the back of his hand. "Don't you dare swear at me or any of my officers! Do you hear?" David was in total shock. He raised both his hands, cupped them over his face, and shook his head from side to side. He then simply answered "I don't know why I'm here!"

Officer Villa started speaking to his colleague in his native tongue for a few minutes, and then there was complete silence. David was so confused. He didn't know what they wanted from him. And then Officer Villa spoke.

"Where is your wife? What have you done with her?" David looked at him in total amazement.

"I don't know what you're talking about. She disappeared and I called you to help me find her. Then I found a note saying that I had to pay one million euros to get her back. That's all I know."

"I know what you did" said Villa. "You think you are so clever, but I can see right through you"

David didn't know what to say, he was bemused. He leaned forward placing both his elbows on the table and put his head in his hands. "Please stop torturing me like this. I don't know what you think I did, but I only want to find my wife. I only want to get my wife back!"

Villa stood up. "I'll tell you what I believe you did." He took off his jacket, started walking around the room, and then started.

"You made up a story that your wife felt she was being stalked all through your holiday. I believe it was you who were stalking her, making her feel she was being watched. This was the first part of your plan. You were planning to kill her, but you didn't have the guts. Not until she humiliated you on that Monday morning, when she shouted at you in the hotel foyer, in front of staff and guests alike. That must have made you feel so small. You also still had it in your mind that she had tried to kill you, by pushing you in front of a car in Naples. You were just waiting for the right moment, and then you would strike!"

If this hadn't been such a serious situation, David would have burst out laughing, but instead he just sat in his chair in complete bewilderment.

Villa continued, "I believe you had been drinking with your wife, and an argument started. In my officer's report, he said you had been drinking whisky. In the middle of that argument your wife stormed off, but you didn't follow her immediately. You made up that silly story that she was going for a doughnut! You stayed in the foyer, seated on your comfortable chair, so that people would notice you....

give you an alibi. That's when you spoke to Senor Martinez, but after he left the hotel you then went to look for your wife. You found her, and during a continuation of the argument you killed her, and then disposed of the body. You came back to the hotel, looking a mess according to Maria. That was because your wife had fought back, but Maria didn't know that. It was then that you came up with the idea that your wife was missing, and that you had been running all over the place trying to find her. That explained your dishevelled appearance. You weren't too happy with the story that your wife had just disappeared, so you had to come up with something else to deflect her disappearance away from you. You placed a note in your 'stolen' luggage bag, that suggested that someone had kidnapped your wife, and were demanding one million euros for her return. Conveniently, you had a witness, Maria, who saw you taking the note from the bag, supposedly for the first time. Was that coincidence? I don't think so! You used Maria! The only fingerprints on that note were yours! Since then, there has been no contact from any kidnappers, because I don't think there were ever any. I believe it was a hoax created by you. All I have to do now is find some evidence to prove all of this, and then you will be going to jail for a very long time. I can't charge you yet, but you will be staying here for at least tonight. Do you have anything to say?"

"Can I speak to Assistant Chief Ramirez?"

"No you can't. You know his wife died on Tuesday night, the same night your wife disappeared, so I don't know when he will be back at work."

"Do you have anything else to say?"

David steeled himself before he answered. He knew what was coming.

"Yes. This is all fucking bullshit!"

Officer Villa punched him on the chin, sending him and his chair across the tiny room.

"I warned you about your language. Someone will be here shortly, to show you to your room for tonight. We'll see you again tomorrow."

Chapter 56

If David thought the first room was dirty, then it was like a palace compared to the one he now found himself in, and he would have to sleep here tonight. The paint was peeling off the walls, but some of the spaces were covered with human faeces, as well as some parts of the floor. Some of it was fresh. Someone had taken D.I.Y. to a new level. The smell was disgusting, a mixture of all human waste.... urine, vomit and shit. The only thing in the room was a wooden bed with a one inch thick mattress, and one thick coarse blanket. David decided to try and make the best of it, so he lay down, and covered himself from head to toe with the blanket, trying to block out the nauseating smell. After a while it worked, and unbelievably he actually fell asleep. He had been through a hell of a time in the last few days, and his body couldn't take any more. It had to shut down for a while to recharge itself. He slept for hours. He didn't know for how long, because there were no windows in the room, and only one fluorescent light, which had been on since he entered the room.

After his sleep, David got up and started walking around the room.... he preferred to think on his feet. He felt so very, very lonely, as if everyone in the world had deserted him. Even beings from a higher level weren't helping him, though God knew that he had prayed for assistance. Up until now, his mind had been consumed by the disappearance of Louise, but now he would have to think about himself. He was in a terrible situation, but he knew that they couldn't keep him in that jail forever. He knew they wouldn't find any evidence, because there was none to be found. He didn't write any ransom note. He didn't kill or kidnap his wife, so how could he be charged for such a crime.

Five minutes later Officer Fernandez opened the cell door, and handed David some sandwiches and a plastic cup full of water. He really didn't think that David should be in this position, but he had to obey his orders, so he couldn't really help him.

"Do you want anything else, like a coffee or a cup of tea?" he asked.

"No thank you officer, but I would like to make one phone call, if that is possible? The only problem is that I don't know the number of the hotel, it's in my mobile phone."

"That's not a problem. You are allowed a phone call. I will be back in ten minutes to collect your cup and plate. I will bring your mobile with me."

Officer Fernandez's ten minutes turned out to be one hour, but David didn't waste that time, he put it to good use. He had to figure out some kind of way to get out of that jail. He couldn't do anything to help himself while he was locked up. He had to come up with a plan. If the truth be told, certain things had taken place over the previous few years that led him to believe that something like this was going to happen.... ever since that first e-mail. He just didn't know when, and for the last year he had been formulating a plan in his mind, well a framework at least. And now he was about to put it into action. He would have to be flexible, and he knew the plan would have to be changed along the way, but this is where it would begin.

As David scrolled down the telephone numbers in his mobile, looking for the Hotel Sants, he asked Officer Fernandez if it was still Sunday, and if so, what time it was.

"It's Sunday night, and it's half past ten" replied Fernandez.

David thanked Fernandez, turned away from him, into the opposite corner of the room and then pressed the call button on his mobile.

"Good evening, could I speak to Maria Lopez please." David had to wait for a moment until Maria came to take his call. "Hi Maria.... it's David Telfer here. I don't know if you know, but I am in jail."

"Yes, I'd heard. That's all the staff have been talking about, how you were basically dragged from the hotel this morning. Are you alright? Was it Officer Villa's doing?"

"Yes, it was, and I'm okay, but I need a favour. Do you know when the funeral ceremony for Assistant Chief Ramirez's wife is taking place?"

"Yes I do. Senor Martinez was telling me that it's tomorrow morning. Although it's only for family, he has been invited, as he has been a friend of the family for such a long time. So what is this favour you want done?"

"Senor Ramirez has helped me since I came to Barcelona....first with the bag incident, and until the unfortunate death of his wife, with the disappearance of Louise. I would like to offer my condolences in the shape of flowers and a Mass card. Could you possibly arrange that for me, please Maria, and just add it onto my bill? Send it by messenger tomorrow morning."

"Yes, that won't be a problem David. But can't you do it yourself when you come back to the hotel?"

"That's the problem, Maria, I'm being kept here in jail for tonight at least, and maybe a lot longer, so I don't know when I'll be back. I really do appreciate your help. Goodnight and thank you again."

David handed his phone back to Officer Fernandez and thanked him, and asked if there was any news of his wife. "No news at all, but we still have officers out tonight, looking for her. If I get any news I will let you know immediately." He turned and locked the door behind him.

David had done all he could for tonight. He had started the ball rolling in his quest for freedom. He had sent the Mass card and the flowers to the man he felt could help him get out of jail. But not only that, David had it in his mind that Assistant Chief Ramirez could in fact become his trump card further down the line. Just at that, the light went out, and David lay down to try and get some sleep.

Chapter 57

It was Tuesday, the day after his wife's funeral, and Gilberto Ramirez was sitting alone in his living room, looking at a pile of Mass cards. He was feeling rather emotional, and if the truth be told, he was also feeling sorry for himself. He sat sipping a glass of red wine, wondering how he was going to cope without the woman he had loved and lived with, for the past thirty nine years. What would he do with himself? How would he fill the massive void left in his life, by her sudden death?

He filled himself another glass of red wine, and sought some comfort by starting to read the Mass cards and letters of condolence he had received from friends and family alike. He felt a deep sadness as he read the moving words and verses, and tears started to stream down his face. However after he had read a few of the cards, he was also overcome by feelings of joy. It was such a strange sensation. Sadness because of the passing of his beautiful wife, and yet joy at the same time, because she had touched the hearts of so many people, during her time on this earth. So many people whom she had known in her life, had taken the time to send these touching words of comfort. He realised that he indeed was a lucky man, to have spent so many years with such a lovely lady, and he should actually be celebrating her life rather than mourning it.

It was then that one card in particular caught his eye. It was sent by David Telfer. At that precise moment, he felt a strong connection to him. Here was a man who had also lost his wife, but in a different sense. There was still a possibility that he might find her, but there was a chance that he might never see her again. She could be dead. But what struck him about this card wasn't the beauty of it, or the eloquence of the words within, it was the fact that the man who sent it, although extremely distressed himself, took the time to even give him a thought in his time of sorrow and grief, never mind send a Mass card.

The detective within Ramirez then took over, as he thought about someone other than his wife, for the first time since her death. He wondered how David Telfer was feeling at that time, if he was coping with the stress, and how the case was progressing under Sergeant Villa. Carlos Angel Martinez had told him after the funeral that he had heard that David Telfer had been taken into custody by Officer Villa on Sunday morning, adding that he had been told that Villa suspected Telfer of murdering his wife, Louise. Ramirez hadn't given it much thought at the time, but now as he sat there sipping his wine, he couldn't see how Villa had come to this conclusion, with the evidence on hand. It could be that Sergeant Villa had uncovered new damning evidence that pointed towards murder, but he would have to wait until he returned to work, to find out for himself. He decided there and then, that he would go back to work the very next day. First thing in the morning he would ask Officer Villa to brief him on the Telfer case, and then he would make up his own mind. If he didn't agree with him, and David Telfer was still in custody, he would order his release immediately.

Assistant Chief Ramirez didn't realise it, but David Telfer had already started his subtle strategy of getting him on his side, by sending the card and flowers. He had planted the seeds of sympathy in the mind of Ramirez. It wouldn't be long before David Telfer was back on the streets of Barcelona, searching for his wife.

Chapter 58

It was Wednesday morning, and David had suffered bout after bout of questioning since Sunday, and he didn't expect today to be any different. But he had never deviated from his story.

'Louise had gone for doughnuts. She hadn't returned after half an hour. He had gone looking for her, but couldn't find her. He had returned to the hotel and Maria had helped him to look for her, but they still couldn't find her. Maria had called the police on his behalf. On Wednesday morning he had found the kidnap note, and that was it.'

He couldn't believe it, but it was already one week since he had found that note, and he was no further forward. In fact he had gone backwards—his wife was still missing, and he was in jail, and he believed he was about to be charged with her murder. However David's Archangel Gabriel was in the building that morning, only his name was not Gabriel, it was Gilberto, Assistant Chief Gilberto Ramirez. He had already spoken to Sergeant Villa and listened intently to his evidence and views on the case of Louise Telfer. He told Ramirez that he suspected David Telfer as soon as he produced the kidnap note in front of the witness, Maria Lopez. From there he had pieced together the case against him, from the stalking on the cruise, to the argument in the hotel, and then the disappearance itself.

When Villa had finished presenting his case to Ramirez, the assistant chief pondered for a few moments, and then asked, "Do you have any concrete evidence to support this? For instance, you say they were arguing in the hotel directly before she disappeared, do you have a witness who saw them? You say he went looking for her and actually found her, and then started arguing again in the street. Have you found anyone who saw them? Do you think he had the opportunity and enough time to murder her in the street, and then find somewhere to dispose of the body, in a city that he doesn't know?" There was silence in the assistant chief's office. Sergeant Villa couldn't answer any of the questions, but after a moment said, "What about the fingerprints on the note. The only prints on it were his?"

"Anyone could have written it. They only had to wear gloves. He had a witness who saw him pulling the note from the bag, so his prints had to be on it."

The sergeant shook his head and answered. "That's what made me suspicious in the first place.

Just give me some time, sir, and I will find the evidence."

Ramirez stood up and began to walk around the room....not saying a single word. Sergeant Villa sat in his chair facing across his boss's desk. The only noise in the room was the clacking of Ramirez's heels against the wooden floor, as he walked behind him, and then back around the desk to his own black leather chair.

Finally, Ramirez spoke, "I will give you all the time you want to find some evidence, but you can't keep David Telfer in custody. You don't have any evidence against the man. In fact, I am sure you are wrong, but I will keep an open mind. In the meantime, release him."

Sergeant Villa then upped and left the room to go and reluctantly release David Telfer, while Assistant Chief Ramirez flipped through the file in front of him. He liked Sergeant Villa, and knew that he was a good officer, but in this case he didn't agree with him for one very good reason.

He knew the truth.

Chapter 59

David stepped out of the police station into the hot Barcelona sun, and for the first time since Louise had disappeared, he felt good. Good, because he was free. Good, because he had escaped that stinking, nauseating, revolting and claustrophobic tiny police cell, where he had spent the last three nights. Good, because he could now re-focus on finding his wife. Good, because he could now have a long, hot, soapy bubble bath. He felt so dirty, not only in body, but also in mind. He asked himself how someone could possibly think he could have killed his wife.

He walked back to the hotel, looking all around him, hoping that he would catch a glimpse of Louise.... he knew he was grasping at straws, but he was desperate. He reached the Hotel Sants, (without seeing Louise), and walked past reception, looking straight ahead. He didn't want to talk to anyone, not even Maria. He took the elevator to the fifth floor, went to his room and turned on the hot water bath tap, pouring some bubble bath soap under the flow of water. He opened the mini bar and took out a small bottle of red wine, unscrewed the top and placed it on the ledge of the bath. He undressed, turned on the cold water tap and tested the water....it was just right. He stepped into the hot bath, laid his head against the back of the bath and sipped his wine. He needed this. He needed to recharge his batteries. He needed to think what he should do next.

What happened next was not what he was thinking.

He heard the room door open and someone walking towards the bathroom...clack, clack, clack, clack...the sound of high heels against the tiled floor.

"Louise? Is that you? Louise?"

David was shaking and tried to grab the bath towel and scramble to his feet at the same time. He was in too much of a rush, and he fell back into the bath. He tried to push up with his right foot, left foot, right, left, right, left, right, left. He couldn't get up. His feet just kept slipping away from under him. He tried to struggle to his feet. He couldn't, he was too excited. One moment later he was flat on his back, the water flapping all around him, and there before him stood a beautiful woman dressed only in her black thong and high heels.

"I hope no one saw you coming into the room! How did you get up here without anyone seeing you?" asked a disbelieving David.

"I came up the back stairs. Are you not pleased to see me?

Moments later they were both entwined in the hot soapy bubbles!

Part 3

Chapter 60

It had been a week since David's release and he had relentlessly trudged around Barcelona's streets, day and night, looking for Louise. He had been warned by Assistant Chief Ramirez,

"Barcelona is a dangerous city. Leave it to us. If she's still in the city, we will find her," he had said.

But David couldn't just sit there in the hotel and do nothing.....he had to feel that he was doing something useful. So, early that evening, he found himself in Las Ramblas, showing his photographs of Louise to anyone who would take the time to look at them. It became so depressing and disheartening. He would offer the pictures to passers by, but they would just walk on and shake their heads. That was until he approached two young men standing at the corner of a small side street which made up part of the red light district, not far from the main boulevard.

"I wonder if either of you can help me? I'm trying to find my wife. This is a photo of her....have you ever seen her before?"

The taller of the two took the picture from David, and started to speak to his friend in Spanish. After a few moments the shorter of the two men spoke to David in broken English. "My friend says he see this woman....ten minutes since."

David's heart jumped!

He could feel the blood pumping through every vein in his body. There was a pounding in his chest, as if someone was beating on it from the inside. His head throbbed. It was the body's reaction to this startling news. But he had to calm himself down, and think what to do next. This man could be mistaken. 'Calm down' he thought to himself, as he took several deep breaths, sucking air in through his nose, and blowing it out through his mouth.

"Can you show me where you saw her?" he asked the man excitedly. The shorter man translated David's words, and then spoke to his friend, again in Spanish. "Si," he answered, "come, follow!"

David couldn't take this all in. He really believed he was going to see Louise again. He would turn the next corner and she would be there.....walking towards him, still dressed in the same clothes she had been wearing when she disappeared. He couldn't wait. He started to run and gestured to his two guides to do the same. "Is it far?" David asked anxiously.

"Not far," the shorter man answered. A few minutes later, he pointed down the street and shouted to David, "next corner, she there!"

They were now deep into the heart of Barcelona. There were no tourists here, unless they really wanted to be. It was very quiet, but it had its attraction for some men. The only people he could see were woman, standing on the street corners, obviously looking for business, but trade seemed to be slack this evening.

Then the shorter man suddenly stopped running. "Just round next corner...your lady there!" he said while the taller one rounded the corner a few steps ahead of them. David had a picture of Louise engrained in his mind....a picture that was about to come to life again. A few more steps and he would be able to touch her again, to hug her, to hold her in his arms He'd found her all by himself, without the help of the police. His whole body was trembling!

Then he turned the corner and WHAM! He felt a huge force explode onto his face, and he was knocked backwards onto the hard pavement. The taller of the two had punched him on the face, and was now kicking him repeatedly, while the short one kneed him in the back, pinned his neck to the ground with his right elbow, and held a knife to his throat.

"Give me all of your fucking money!" Amazingly he could now speak perfect English.

David was so disorientated, that he couldn't even make out what the thugs were saying. They continued to reign blows down on him, thinking that he was ignoring them. The smaller one dug his hand deep into David's pockets, ripping them in the process. All he could find was one twenty euro note...David's funds were getting low. They then both gave him one last kick each, and walked away arguing with each other.

He lay there for a few moments, before slowly turning onto his stomach, groaning as he did so. He placed his hands in the press-up position, summoned all of his strength together, and pushed himself up onto his feet. He gingerly made his way back to the hotel, thinking all the while that he should have listened to Gilberto Ramirez's warning. However his wife was still missing and he wasn't going to let this incident put him off.

Only moments before he had felt the furore swell within him, when he thought he had found Louise. What a feeling that had been, and he wouldn't give up until he found her. He would just have to be more careful in the future, and protect himself better.

Right then and there he decided, 'I'm going to get myself a gun!'

Chapter 61

Back at the hotel, Maria was standing at reception when David walked in through the door. She was stunned. His shirt was torn, his trousers ripped, and he was limping badly.

"What happened to you? Don't tell me! You were beaten up and robbed. I told you, Barcelona is a very dangerous city!"

David still hadn't lost his sense of humour.

"You should have seen the other guy!" he quipped.

"I don't know how you can joke about it. You could have been killed!"

"I'm sorry, but I'm just so fed up. I was just trying to cheer myself up a bit, and anyway I'm okay. But it won't stop me searching for Louise. The only thing is, I don't know what to do next!"

"Well I can help you there. You can clean yourself up, get changed, and meet Assistant Chief Ramirez in the Italian restaurant across the street, at half past eight. He came in to see you, but as you weren't here, he left you an invite for dinner. He wants to talk to you....about a new lead."

From feeling so down moments before, David was now on a high. Not only because there was a new lead, but because Assistant Chief Ramirez was obviously feeling a little sorry for him and that could prove useful in David's future plans.

Chapter 62

Assistant Chief Ramirez was already seated at a small table in the corner of the restaurant, when David limped in. As he entered, David waved to Ramirez, and was then shown to his seat by one of the waiters.

"What happened to you?" asked Ramirez, as he watched David struggle to sit down. He also couldn't help but notice the swelling on the left side of his face, and the cut below his right eye. David then explained what had happened to him earlier that evening, and then had to listen to Ramirez ranting at him, because he hadn't listened to his warning. The waiter saved him from any more verbal punishment, when he approached the table and asked them what they would like to eat.

David seized the opportunity. "I'll have the penne carbonara, please." Assistant Chief Ramirez answered the waiter in his native tongue, but David, even with his limited knowledge of the Spanish language, understood his order. Spaghetti bolognaise and a bottle of the best red wine in the house. The waiter turned and walked away, and David took the chance to change the thread of the conversation.

"I was really sorry to hear about your wife. You must be devastated, and it was so sudden. I do understand how you feel at the moment, even although I might get my Louise back...oh I'm so sorry, that was really insensitive of me. Here I am babbling on, depressing you, but I don't mean to. I just feel such a strong connection with you and your circumstances at the moment. I'm sorry."

Gilberto Ramirez had to admit to himself that he actually did relate to David Telfer's present predicament, and did feel a connection with this man he hardly knew. After all they had both lost their wives on exactly the same day. However he had to be professional, he couldn't get too close to him and let his feelings cloud his judgement. He changed the subject.

"We're working on a new theory. That's why I invited you to dinner.... to tell you all about it, and to ask you a few questions. I thought this would be much more civilised than your last question and answer session. I'm sorry about that. Officer Villa is a good policeman, but he can be a little over zealous at times."

The waiter then brought over their meals, and opened the bottle of wine he had previously set down on the table. He poured a little into the Assistant Chief's glass and waited for him to try it. He tasted the wine and nodded his approval. Enrique, the waiter, as one could tell from his name badge on his lapel, filled both of their glasses, and wished them the obligatory 'enjoy your meal', then left them to their pasta.

"Have you had any contact from anyone, other than that first ransom note, regarding your wife?" started Ramirez.

"Not a thing. I can't sleep, I can't eat....in fact this is my first proper meal for days. I just don't know what to do, except to keep looking for her, and waiting and hoping for some sort of contact from her or her captors, if she has indeed been kidnapped."

"We now believe that this is indeed the case...your wife has been kidnapped."

"Officer Villa doesn't seem to think so!"

"I have spoken to him, and now, how you say in English? We are both singing from the same hymn sheet. Is that correct?"

"Yes, that's right. Well I'm glad to hear that. I can now relax a little, knowing that I'm no longer a suspect. Does that mean I am now allowed to leave Barcelona? Not that I want to leave just yet!"

"Yes you can, and although I know that you won't want to, you will soon have to think about carrying on with your own life, getting back to your own life in your own country."

"I haven't even thought about that yet. I can only think of Louise."

Assistant Chief Ramirez nodded his head knowingly, and then continued with his theory.

"As I have said already, we believe that she has been kidnapped. In the last few years, there has been a spate of what we call 'secuestro express'--- 'express kidnapping'. We call it that, because they are planned very quickly. They are opportune thieves. They 'steal' people and then demand money. It happens all of the time in South American countries like Brazil and Columbia, and we believe it started here a few years ago in Spain, Madrid to be precise, due to the influx of people from that part of the world. However, having said that, we think that your wife's case is different, in that she has been kidnapped by locals."

David had stopped eating. He sat with both elbows on the table, hands clasped in front of him, totally astounded by this startling new information.

"What makes you think that?" he asked.

"The theft of your bag!"

"I don't understand" added David in a questioning tone.

"We believe that the thieves who stole your bag were also the ones who 'stole' your wife. They took your travel documents, and from the information on the hotel invoice and cruise ship boarding pass, they simply delved into your lives. For instance your passport number is there for all to see, and they basically used such information to retrieve all sorts of details about you and your wife. We believe that they discovered that your wife was quite a successful model in her younger days, found pictures of her through the internet, in glossy magazine photo shoots, and decided that you must be rich. That's how these people work...they see an opportunity to make money and they take it. We have about fifty such cases on record, with many more not even recorded, and the victims come from all walks of lives. They have taken loved ones of lawyers, doctors, pop stars, film stars, sports stars, and property developers, but they all had one thing in common....they were rich. Normally the kidnappers ask for relatively small amounts of money... fifty to a hundred thousand euros. In most of the cases, the victim's families have actually paid the ransom money... firstly, because they wanted the return of their loved ones, and secondly because they didn't want the whole thing publicised."

"And what happened?" asked David anxiously.

"The victim was returned unharmed, in most of the cases."

"What about the other cases?"

"Some were found only days after they were kidnapped, with no ransom paid. And in three of the cases, I'm afraid the victims are still on the missing person list. But as I have said already, we believe that this case is different. We think they are local thieves who are just chancing their arm. In all of these recorded 'express kidnappings', no one has ever asked for one million euros. We also believe that the young man who returned your bag, was the same one who stole it. We think he is part of the gang of kidnappers, and that he put the note into your bag. "

"How do you know that?"

"Just trust me, I know."

David cupped his two hands around his face, and just sat there, staring at Gilberto. After a moment's silence he took his hands away and said,

"I don't believe this. It's all too simple!"

"It is simple. I didn't have the information that these people had, but earlier today I simply googled your wife's name, and there was her portfolio. She looked like a million dollars, and that's what these people saw---a chance to make money---one million euros as it said on the note." David was confused. He knew that the person who returned his bag was dead. How could he possibly have taken Louise?

"You will have to explain to me how they kidnapped her. And please answer me this. If you know who stole my bag, why haven't you arrested them?"

"That's where the problems begin!" answered Ramirez.

Chapter 63

Maria was working at the reception desk when he walked through the revolving doors into the hotel foyer. She pretended she didn't see him as she fed the names of her new guests into the computer. She kept her eyes on the screen hoping that he would speak to someone else, and let her get on with her work. She hated him.

She hated the way he stripped her naked with his eyes, every time he looked at her.

She hated the way he patted her backside every time he passed behind her.

She hated the way he pretended to fix her shirt collar and then allowed his hand to brush 'accidentally' against her breast.

She hated the way he had cheated on his wife for so many years, although it was said that his mistress for the past few years was the 'real thing', and it was rumoured he was going to divorce his wife for her.

She hated the way he arrogantly walked about the hotel as if he owned it, but the fact of the matter was that he did!

"Buenas noches Maria" said Carlos Angel Martinez as he walked around behind Maria. Right on cue, he patted her ass.

"Good evening Senor Martinez." She wondered if he could see her clenched teeth from behind her. A shiver ran down her spine. She loved her work, but she hated the impromptu visits of her boss.

"Is there any news on the Telfer kidnapping? Have the kidnappers made any contact yet?"

"Not as far as I know sir. All I know is that Mr. Telfer has been walking the streets, showing people photographs of his wife, hoping that someone recognises her. So far he's had no luck."

"What about Assistant Chief Ramirez? Do you know if he is back on the case?"

"Yes he is, sir. He came in earlier, looking for Mr. Telfer, who was actually out searching for his wife at the time. They are now both in the Italian restaurant across the street, having dinner. Senor Ramirez wanted to speak to him about a new lead in the case. Why don't you go across and see them, sir?"

Maria crossed her fingers, toes, legs and everything else she could possibly cross, hoping that he would take her suggestion on board.

"No, I don't think so. It's really got nothing to do with me. The only connection I have with this whole scenario is that Mrs Telfer was abducted from outside one of my hotels, while staying as a guest. I don't think that entitles me to force myself upon them, when Assistant Chief Ramirez is bringing Mr Telfer up to date with the latest developments. But I have to admit I do feel sorry for him. He has come to Barcelona on holiday, had his bag stolen, and then had his wife kidnapped by the looks of things. That's some holiday!"

"I know. He must be devastated" Maria replied.

She thought she was seeing a different side of Senor Martinez. He genuinely looked as if he did feel some compassion for David Telfer and his present situation. She had never before seen her boss showing any sympathy for anyone. Could this be the new Carlos Martinez?

One moment later, the old Carlos returned.

"How many nights has he stayed free gratis?"

"That's two weeks sir."

"That's ok, but we'll just have to keep an eye on the situation, he can't stay here 'free' for ever. In the meantime,

I'm off home, but if you find out anything, please call me on my mobile. Buenas noches."

He was staying in his home in Sitges, a small city about thirty five kilometres southwest of Barcelona, where property prices were as expensive as even the major European cities. But he didn't want anyone to know that house, and he never gave anyone that telephone number. It was his secret hideaway.

Maria smiled as she bid Senor Martinez goodnight, glad that his flying visit was over...she could relax again. Her shift was almost over and she could go home and chill out with a glass of wine. But it was at times like this that she didn't really like going home to an empty house. She would have preferred to have someone to talk to when she arrived home....a husband, a partner, to share a bottle of wine with, and talk about the day's goings on.

She hadn't given up on finding her Mr Right, her own Don Juan, to sweep her off her feet and take her away from all of this. She dreamed about travelling the world with her knight in shining armour. He would take her away from all of this, and she wouldn't need to endure her boss's visits any longer. She could tell Carlos Angel Martinez that she didn't need his job any more, and he could stick it where the 'sun don't shine'.

However in the meantime she would have to wait. But she had the feeling that that moment in time was getting closer and closer......she would just have to be patient, and she would find him.

Chapter 64

Alfonso Pique was fifty two years old, stood six feet tall and was of medium build. He was an Elliot Gould lookalike with his tousled greying hair, and a moustache and a beard to match. When he wore his thin black rimmed glasses, and his brown tweed jacket with the leather elbow pads, he looked every inch like a college lecturer. He was a likeable soul who had worked in the Hotel Sants for the past fifteen years. Even after all that time, most of the staff really didn't know him. He was a quiet man who kept himself to himself.

He didn't have many friends outside of work either, and he lived alone in a small flat on the outskirts of the city. He had never married, but he had enjoyed several relationships over the years, just like any normal red blooded male. However he had never found that special one, partly due to the fact that he didn't really trust woman. One woman who he did trust was Maria Lopez. When she started work in the Hotel Sants six years ago, they immediately hit it off. She was a very beautiful woman, but it wasn't her looks that attracted him, it was the fact that she was so easy to talk to. He now considered her a real friend. That's why he took the time to speak to David Telfer about Juan Marquez when Maria had asked him. If she trusted this man, then that was good enough for him. He considered Maria to be a great judge of character.

He was sitting in the Cafe Magic having a coffee and a cigarette that night, as he always did, before he started his night shift at nine o'clock. It was his usual routine. Half an hour before he was due to start his work, he would take his seat at the same table on the cafe terrace, and just watch the world go by. Tonight he was thinking about his own life and how everything was going so well up until Juan's death. He had not only lost a friend but also the big cash payout he had been expecting to receive for their last 'hit'. Alfonso was in a lot of debt, but he had been gradually paying it off with the help of the blackmailing scam he ran with Juan Marquez. Now he would have to find some other way of getting the money. He would certainly miss Juan Marquez!

It was just then that he noticed David Telfer limping across the road.

"Mr Telfer" he called, but David didn't hear him as he headed for Luigi's Italian restaraunt.

He shouted out once more, "Mr Telfer!"

He wanted to ask David if he had any luck in the search for his wife, as he genuinely felt sorry for him, but once again he didn't hear him. However that wasn't the only reason why he wanted to speak to him. He wanted to know what the police were saying about this whole episode.

Alfonso was feeling a little more than anxious about his involvement in all of this business. He was beginning to think he had made a mistake in telling David about the little operation he had going with Juan Marquez, and he feared that he might tell the police. If they found out about his blackmailing activities, they would surely delve into his past. It wouldn't be long before they not only discovered that he was up to his eyes in debt, but that he also had a criminal record.

As an eighteen year old he had spent two years in jail for aggravated burglary. That was a long time ago, but he knew as soon as the police found out, they would try and pin everything on him....the bag theft, the murder of Juan Marquez, because he was sure that he had been murdered, and finally blame him for the disappearance of Louise.

But something was puzzling him about this case. So much had happened at the hotel in the past few weeks and yet the police hadn't even questioned him once. That didn't seem like normal police procedure.

'It was as if they weren't looking for the answers' he thought to himself. 'Or maybe they think they have all the answers and are building a case against someone....tying up all the loose ends before they strike!' He gave up on that train of thought, finished his coffee and made his way towards Luigi's.

He couldn't see through the smoked glass door, so he popped his head in and tried to see where David was sitting. The restaurant was quite busy and he couldn't pick him out on his first sweep. However seconds later he noticed David seated at a table in the corner of the room, with another man. He couldn't see his face at first, but as he turned side on to talk to one of the waiters, he recognised him as the Assistant Chief of Police, Gilberto Ramirez. He and David looked as if they were having a very cosy tete-a-tete. Alfonso went weak at the knees!

All of his previous thoughts came rushing back into his head! Was David telling Ramirez about his blackmailing scam? Was he the one they were building a case against? He quickly turned round and slammed the door shut. He didn't want them to see him.

He stood with his back to the door, leaning his head against the top glass panel, thinking about what he should do next. His heart was pounding. He took several deep breaths and then slowly walked across the street to the hotel, taking his jacket off as he crossed the road. He had been planning to take a short holiday after he had received his cash handout from Juan, but obviously that was now a non starter. The only holiday he could see for himself now was an extended stay in a prison cell.

Alfonso knew he had a big decision to make. If he stayed in Barcelona, the police would question him again and again, and probably make his life a misery. But if he suddenly disappeared, they would definitely take that as a sign of guilt. But he wasn't guilty of anything!

In fact, as far as he knew, the police didn't have any evidence to say that any crime had been committed at all. Right there and then he decided he would put his trust in David Telfer, who had sworn to him that he would never tell a soul about his money making scheme.

His mind was made up.

He was going nowhere.

Chapter 65

Enrique approached the table, asked if they were enjoying their meal, and if they wanted anything else. Assistant Chief Ramirez shook his head and continued with his theory.

"Emilio Torres was the name of the man who returned your bag to the hotel. I believe that he also stole it with the help of his friend, Eduardo Salgado. They were working in tandem with a man that you have already met, Emilio's uncle, Juan Marquez, your witness to the theft. When they took your bag, they were obviously hoping to make a killing, but as you know they didn't get much, so that's when they came up with the idea of the 'express kidnapping' of Louise. However by the time it came to the kidnapping, all three of them were dead."

David was shocked. He knew of two of the deaths, but to hear of another death in connection with his bag theft was just so hard to take in....in fact all of this information was beginning to overwhelm him. "So, who kidnapped Louise?"

"We believe there must be a fourth member of the gang, who actually went through with the kidnapping, but we don't know who it is. That's what we're working on at the moment, but we think that he or she is probably the weakest member of the outfit, and they have taken cold feet.... that's the reason they haven't made any further contact. Usually with this type of 'secuestro express', the perpetrators make contact very quickly. If we are right about this, then we really do need to hear from him or her as soon as possible. I must be honest with you... the longer we go without any sort of contact, then I'm afraid the slimmer the chances of finding your wife."

"What are you saying? What will they do with Louise?"

"I'm afraid that the most likely outcome is that she would be sold into the sex trade industry, as she is a very beautiful woman, and would attract quite a high price. That would be the easiest way out, for the mystery kidnapper. They would get some money, and wouldn't be in any danger of getting caught by us. However my next move is to get a photo of your wife in the local papers along with a short story of what has happened, and hopefully we will get some feedback. "

David sat in silence. Was Gilberto Ramirez's theory right? Was he telling him the truth? Did the Assistant Chief really believe that Louise had been kidnapped? Was there indeed a fourth member of a kidnap gang? Or was Ramirez not telling him the full story, and in fact hiding something?

David didn't know what to believe, but he couldn't help thinking about the fourth gang member theory. When the Assistant Chief had mentioned this, David had immediately thought of Alfonso, who had already admitted to him that he was involved in a scam with Juan Marquez. Could he be involved in something more sinister, like a kidnapping? He didn't say anything to Senor Ramirez, but made up his mind that he would confront Alfonso himself, and then decide what he would do. He thanked Senor Ramirez for the meal and then excused himself saying that he was exhausted and he would have to go to bed and get some sleep.

"I will think about everything you have told me, and see if I can recollect any small detail I may have forgotten. I will also consider my own position, and decide what I am going to do next. In the meantime, I must thank you for the meal, Senor Ramirez, and for all your help."

"Please, call me Gilberto. And as for everything else, I'm only doing my job. I'll be in touch soon. Buenas noches."

David answered goodnight and then turned and walked out of the restaurant. As he turned, a smile spread across his face. He couldn't believe that everything was happening so quickly. He was already on first name terms with the Assistant Chief of Police of Barcelona, and he might have to turn to him for help in the future, if things did not turn out the way he was expecting.

Chapter 66

David woke up next day at noon..... he couldn't believe he had slept for so long. He lay in bed looking up at the ceiling, thinking of everything that had happened on this holiday, and about his conversation with Gilberto the previous evening. He wondered what could possibly have happened to Louise. Where could she be? How long could he afford to stay in Barcelona? How long would it be before his boss phoned him and asked him to return to his work? What would he do next? He just lay there, deciding on his plan of action.

Firstly he would speak to Maria about Alfonso, and suss out her thoughts on whether she thought he was capable of kidnapping Louise. Then again, he thought to himself, Gilberto had mentioned in his theory that the fourth gang member could be a woman. What about Maria? What about Maria and Alfonso? There was no reason why there couldn't be five in the gang.

He stared up into space, not really seeing anything. His mind was suddenly blank. Then one mili-second later, he snapped out of it.

There was no way that Maria was involved in this, she had helped him from the minute he had entered the hotel. She had even searched the streets for Louise the night she had disappeared. He trusted her, and not only that, he had known her from the last time he had visited Barcelona, when she had also helped him. But, as for Alfonso.... he didn't know him at all. He had only spoken to him once, so for all he knew he could be a mass murderer. He decided that he would shower, get dressed and go down and speak to Maria.

David turned to get out of bed, but suddenly stopped and let out a painful yell...."aaarrrrrrgh!" With all his focus on what had happened the night before, he completely forgot about the beating he had taken. Every bone in his body ached. He lay half on his left side, half on his back, motionless. Beads of sweat ran down his temples, and he felt faint. He gave himself a couple of minutes to regain his composure, and then slowly dragged himself over to the edge of the bed, where he managed to swing his legs and feet over, until they were hanging over the side of the bed. He pushed himself up with his arms until he was finally sitting up on the bed, with both feet on the floor. He then stood up and slowly walked over to the bathroom and started to run a hot bath for himself. He was glad that he had slept 'au naturel' last night, as he would have found it very difficult to take his pyjamas off this morning.

He lay in that hot bath for half an hour, and was amazed at the difference. He was still in pain, but nothing like it had been earlier. He got out of the bath, got dressed and went down to reception.

He smiled at Maria as he slowly walked across the hotel foyer, trying to hide the pain he was feeling, so that she wouldn't chastise him again for walking the streets of Barcelona after dark, on his own. The smile that he was expecting to receive in return never materialised.

"Where have you been? I was so worried about you. I didn't see you return from the restaurant last night and you looked in so much pain when you left here. And this morning, no one has seen you. I was just about to come up to your room to check on you." Maria looked at David, and waited for an answer.

"You sound just like my wife" he quipped. No sooner had those words left his mouth when he wished he hadn't said them. He realised that this was the first time he had actually said something about his wife in jest since her disappearance. He somehow felt a terrible sense of guilt. He shouldn't be joking about his wife. For Christ sake, she was missing.

Maria noticed his discomfort and smiled at him reassuringly.

"I'm sorry Maria, but I didn't think you would be worried about me. I came back from Luigi's last night and went straight to my bed. I was so tired. As for this morning, I have just woken up, and I have to admit that it took me a little more time than usual to get out of my bed. Every bone in my body aches like hell, and I had to lie in a hot bath for half an hour, to try and ease the pains. At least it has helped a little, and I'm ready to hit the streets again. But I need your help again, Maria. What time do you finish? Can we go somewhere and have a coffee or a beer? I'd like to pick your brains. I also need another favour."

"I don't finish until eight this evening, but I'm free then. I have nothing planned."

"Would you like to go for something to eat then, and we can have a chat?"

"Okay."

David walked towards the hotel door and turned to Maria, saying, "See you at eight" before disappearing through the revolving door, off on yet another search of the streets of Barcelona, hoping to find his wife Louise.

Maria watched David limp along the pavement in front of the huge hotel widow, and wondered what David had meant when he said he would 'like to pick her brains.' She would just have to wait and see, but she had to admit to herself, she was looking forward to it.

Chapter 67

David returned from his search at five o'clock.......
he was sore all over. He decided to soak in another hot
bath for an hour, before his meeting with Maria. He wasn't
going to walk the streets tonight, he had decided. He would
rest for a few days before resuming his search for Louise.
In the meantime he would focus his attention on his 'date'
with Maria and try and find out more about Alfonso. After
his bath, he shaved and put on fresh clothes before calling
reception. It was Maria who answered.

"Are we still alright for tonight Maria?"

Maria recognised David's voice immediately and
answered, "Yes, are you?"

"Sure, I'm just calling to say that I will wait for you in
the Café Magic. I don't think it would look too good if we
left the hotel together. Some people might get the wrong
idea."

"That's fine. See you there." Maria smiled as she
placed the handset back in its cradle... she was feeling
excited!

David put the phone down, splashed on some after-
shave and then left for the café. It was seven thirty.

At the Café Magic, David picked an outside table
and ordered a small beer, while he waited for Maria. He
couldn't help but continually look up and down the street,
hoping that Louise would magically appear, making her
way back to the hotel as if nothing had happened. But it
was not to be.

Maria turned up at ten past eight, and although she
was still wearing her work clothes, she still managed to

look stunning. David stood up and pulled her chair back for her as she approached the table. "Hello Maria, how are you? Would you like a drink here, or would you like to go to another restaurant, and then have a drink?"

"I will have a glass of red wine please David, and if you don't mind, I would like to eat here. I'm feeling a bit tired and I don't want to walk anywhere but home."

"Suits me fine, I'll get a couple of menus."

"I don't need one thanks, I know what I want... a tuna salad."

"Great, I'll have the same." He then ordered up two tuna salads and a bottle of red wine, before starting to tell Maria what Assistant Ramirez had said to him the previous evening.

The waiter appeared with the salads and wine just as David reached the part about the fourth gang member. He stopped to allow the waiter to set down the salads and bread, and to pour the wine. He then continued and asked Maria if she thought Alfonso could possibly be the mysterious missing gang member. Maria was shocked.

"There's no way that Alfonso would be involved in such a thing as kidnapping. I've known him for years, and he isn't capable of that."

"That's why I wanted to talk to you away from the hotel Maria. I didn't want to get Alfonso into any sort of trouble. But I don't know him, so I had to ask someone about him, and that's why I'm asking you. He told me about the blackmailing scam he had going with Juan Marquez, so I thought if he was involved with him in blackmail, he may be into something else with him, like this 'secuestro express.' The Assistant Chief is adamant that Juan Marquez, Emilio Torres and Eduardo Salgado are involved in the kidnapping. But they are all dead."

Maria put her wine down, and David topped up her glass. She nodded her approval and then answered him. "David, I have never heard of Eduardo Salgado, but I do know that Marquez and Torres got the name of being petty thieves, not kidnappers. And although I have heard of these types of kidnappings, I actually don't believe a word of it in this case. Not with the names of the people he has mentioned. If you ask me, I think Assistant Chief Ramirez is grasping at straws."

"I tend to agree with you Maria, that's why I didn't mention Alfonso's name or tell him about his connection with Juan Marquez, when he spoke about the fourth member. You can reassure Alfonso on that count. In fact, I am now getting the feeling that the assistant chief is hiding something from me. It's just a feeling, but I don't think he is telling me everything."

"What are you going to do then?" asked Maria as she finished her salad.

"Well Maria, I plan to keep searching for another two weeks and then I'm going home, with or without Louise. I will have to get back to my work in order to come back here as many times as I can, and I can't do that without money, so I have to keep earning. I will keep in touch with Gilberto and he will notify me if there are any new developments while I am back home in Scotland."

"Oh! Gilberto?" said Maria with a light hearted, sarcastic tone to her voice. "Are you on first name terms with the Assistant Chief already?"

"As a matter of fact I am, but only because he lost his own wife exactly the same day that Louise disappeared, and he seems to sympathise with the predicament I find myself in. Enough about that, let's move on to the other reason I asked you here. I need to ask you for a favour."

"Ask me then" said Maria, who was dying to know what he wanted.

"I've just told you that I'm going to keep searching the streets for another two weeks, and you have already warned me how dangerous that can be at night time. I discovered that for myself last night, when I was jumped upon and beaten. Well I'm certainly not going to stop searching, but I would feel better protected if I had a gun, and you've already told me that you have your brother's gun. So, I'm asking you if you would lend it to me. I know it's asking a lot, but I'm desperate!"

The silence was deafening.

"Do you know how to even fire a gun?" Maria eventually asked.

"As a matter of fact I do, I was once in a gun club back home, when we lived in Stirling."

What happened next took David completely by surprise!

Maria, who was feeling quite tipsy now, quietly said, "If that's the case, then you can have the gun. But I'm not bringing it into the hotel, you will have to come to my flat to get it...it's not far from here."

She then leaned across the table and kissed him full on the lips. David didn't pull away, but when she stopped, he glared at her and said, "Maria, don't ever do that again! The police are looking for my kidnapped wife, and you are kissing me in public. What if someone saw us and decided to tell the police? What will they think? I'll see you tomorrow."

David then got up, put enough money on the table to pay the bill, and left Maria sitting by herself in the Café Magic.

As he lay in bed that night, he couldn't get that kiss out of his mind!

Chapter 68

David woke up the next morning at seven. He hardly slept a wink. He was still every bit as sore as the previous day, so he had to go through the same procedure as the day before.....struggle to get out of bed, and then lie in a hot bath for an hour. It was almost nine when he heard the knock at the door. On answering, he was greeted by a young bellboy who handed him a package, then immediately turned and scampered. David turned the parcel looking for an address or a name, but he couldn't see anything. He then held it up to his ear and shook it. No sound came from the oblong shaped box. He wondered if he should call the Assistant Chief, after all it could have been sent from the kidnappers, and he didn't want to contaminate any evidence. He considered his situation for several moments, and then made his decision. He would phone the police.

He was sweating profusely.

What was in the box?

Could it possibly be new instructions from the kidnappers along with one of Louise's fingers or maybe an ear, just to show that they meant business? He had read of such things in the newspapers.

He made his way to the phone, his heart beating wildly, his head throbbing, and the palms of his hands sticky with nervous sweat. He reached out to pick up the handset, when suddenly the telephone rang. His whole body stiffened with fear, and the pain he had been feeling earlier completely disappeared. A few moments later, he slowly lifted the handset, but he didn't say a word. Then he heard a familiar voice from the other end of the line.

"Hello David, are you there? Did you get my parcel?"

David recognised the voice immediately and let out a huge sigh of relief. It was Maria.

"Hello Maria, yes I got it, but you gave me one hell of a fright. I thought it was from the kidnappers, and I was just about to phone Gilberto."

"Oh, I'm so sorry David, I never gave that a thought. I was so ashamed at my behaviour last night that I decided to bring it into work with me, and send it up with the bell-boy. I didn't want to be seen delivering the package personally. As you said last night, people might get the wrong idea."

"I'm glad you can see that now. So, I take it that it's the gun that's in the package."

"Yes. The Glock 17, and once again I apologise for my insensitivity last night. You can return it when you're finished with it, but you won't see me for a few days... I'm taking some time off."

"Apology accepted. I know you now realise your actions could have jeopardised everything. Thanks again for the gun and I will speak to you after you return from your few days off. Have a nice break. By the way, it was a wonderful kiss. Adios."

Chapter 69

It was raining heavily outside, so David made the decision to stay indoors today. He was going to take the day off.....have a complete break from his constant searching. In fact, 'I'll just have tonight off as well', he thought to himself.

He sat down on the sofa, switched on the television, and tried to find an English speaking news channel, like Sky News for instance, to allow him to catch up with world events. He had been so wrapped up with his own problems, that he had lost track of what was going on elsewhere in the big bad world. He had just found Sky News, when he remembered that Assistant Chief Ramirez had told him that he was asking the local papers to print a photograph of Louise.

He had completely forgotten about this and hadn't even bought a paper. He immediately put on his shoes and went downstairs to reception to purchase one. Maria was still there.

"Good morning Maria, I thought you might have gone already."

"No, not yet, I finish at eleven, and then I'm off for a week. I'm looking forward to the break. So, how can I help you David?"

She was sounding really upbeat, now that she had sorted out last night's problem with David, and she was also excited at the thought of her week's holiday.

"I'm looking to buy a couple of local newspapers. Do you have any here?" enquired David.

"No I'm sorry, but there is a newsagent's shop just next to the Café Magic. What papers are you looking for?"

"I don't really know. Gilberto, (he was getting used to calling him by his first name) said he would have an article about Louise's disappearance printed in the local papers, so I was interested in finding out if it was in any of today's editions."

"The newspapers you should buy are the two local Barcelona papers, 'El Mundo Deportivo' and 'La Vanquardia'. They are obviously Spanish papers, so if you want anything translated, just bring them to me, and I will do that for you. But remember, I finish at eleven this morning, so you will have to hurry."

"Thanks again Maria. I'm losing count of how many times I have to say 'thanks' to you. See you in ten minutes."

Sure enough, David was back at reception ten minutes later with both papers. He looked a little disappointed.

"Is everything alright? Have they published her photograph?" asked Maria, on noticing his glum expression.

"Yes, it's in both papers, page eight in this one, and page ten in this one," said David as he lifted up both newspapers. "But look at the size of it! It's tiny!" He showed Maria La Vanquardia. At the bottom of page eight was a small one inch photo of Louise, with about four lines of script below. Maria translated it as:

'Local police are on the lookout for this missing British woman. If anyone has seen her, please call this telephone number.' She didn't read out the number.

The 'El Mundo Deportivo' had exactly the same photograph and wording.

Neither of them was impressed.

"I can't imagine those articles will get us anywhere" said David. "I thought there would be a full story to accompany the photo. What do you think, Maria?"

"I think that it's a complete waste of time. No one will give them a second look, considering where both papers have positioned them" said Maria as she started perusing the other pages.

She suddenly stopped at page two.

"Now, there's a surprise!"

"What's that?" asked David, as he hurriedly moved around behind Maria to look over her shoulder at the paper.

On page two, there was a large photo of Carlos Angel Martinez, accompanied by half inch high headlines. "What does that mean, Maria?" asked David as he pointed at the newspaper.

"Basically it means 'Carlos Angel Martinez leaves the race for Mayor of Barcelona.' It goes on to say that he has had enough of the pressures of both campaigning for Mayor and running a business empire at the same time. The scrutiny of the Spanish media has also taken its toll on both himself and his family, so he feels he has no alternative but to stop his campaign. He will now be taking a complete break for the next month." Maria looked at David.

"I can't believe that! That doesn't sound like the Carlos Martinez that I know. He loves the limelight and the pressures, he thrives on them. There must be something else behind this story. One good thing, I won't see him for at least a month, that suits me just fine!"

David smiled at Maria, as he knew she didn't like Martinez. He didn't know him personally, but having met him, he didn't think he looked the type of man who couldn't handle pressure.

He was one cool looking hombre.

David then thanked Maria again and wished her 'a nice break', before making his way back up to his room. As he turned, he looked at the photograph of Carlos Angel Martinez, and thought that this was another weird twist that he could add to his list of strange and unexpected happenings, that had occurred on this holiday.

At that particular moment, he couldn't help but think, rightly or wrongly, that somehow they were all connected.

Chapter 70

Over the next two days, David only left the hotel once. He went down to the nearest liquor store where he bought a bottle of Glenmorangie malt whisky. In fact, other than that, he only left his hotel room to go to the restaurant for his meals. The rest of the time, he watched television......football, tennis, boxing, world news, anything to pass the time while he recovered from his beating. He also tried to alleviate his aches and pains by taking three hot baths each day, and taking his medicine...Glenmorangie. He liked his medicine!

He also did a lot of thinking, especially at the end of his second day holed up in his room. That Saturday night, as he lay in bed staring up into space, he let his mind drift back to the first time he had met Louise, and back to the 'good times'.

Just one month before he met her, he had been left £130,000 in his aunt's will. He could remember thinking 'how lucky am I?' And then to cap it all, he had met Louise.

Love at first sight. What a month that was!

He had wooed her by taking her to the best restaurants, drinking the best wine and lavishing her with expensive gifts. He took her on exotic holidays or romantic city breaks three or four times a year. She loved it. He loved it. He was so happy. He wanted to be with her 24/7. He could remember thinking to himself 'this is it, this is the one'.

He proposed. She accepted.

A tear ran down his cheek as he remembered that joyous moment... a single tear of joy.

And then there was THE wedding. Louise had wanted such a lavish wedding. She always wanted the best, and he had given her what she wanted. He could see her in his mind's eye, standing at the altar by his side, in her beautiful wedding dress. He closed his eyes and visualised their first dance together at the luxury hotel, situated on the bonny banks of Loch Lomond. It was a wonderful day, the best day of his life. Louise was so considerate, kind, gentle and loving in those days, he remembered, and she loved life.

She loved going on holiday, as did he. She loved shopping, at that time, and he smiled as he remembered her falling through the front door of their home, laden with parcels. She loved eating out at the best restaurants, drinking the best wine, and going out socialising. And he loved the fact that she could do all of those things in those days, due to the money that he had inherited.

Then the smile left his face as he remembered when it had all changed.

Louise had lost a baby, and she had become a different person.

As he lay there reminiscing, thinking of the striking change in Louise, a thought suddenly leapt into his head. That wasn't the only dramatic event that had occurred around that time.

It was a Saturday afternoon and Louise had been out shopping again, and for the first time ever, her credit card was refused. She had been livid, and threatened to get the young assistant sacked. She had told her to try it again, which the young girl did, but it was no use. There was no money left in that account. She had come home and torn strips off David, but there was nothing he could do. They had spent all of the inheritance money. No, not 'they', she had spent all of the money! They couldn't go on holiday, and they had to stop eating out at the best restaurants. That was when Louise really changed.

For the first time in his life, it struck David that the end of the 'good times' had coincided with the end of the money. David had always been blinded by his love for Louise when it came to seeing any faults in her, even though they might be staring him in the face. He was now beginning to think that maybe Louise had played him for a fool all of these years. She had treated him badly for many years during her 'depression', and he had just taken it all. He felt the anger bubble up inside his stomach as he began to realise that he had been used. Louise had used him to cater for her every whim. He worked, she didn't. He went home from work, did all the housework and even made her dinner. She didn't lift a finger. He gently coaxed her back into normal life, and eventually back to work as a model.

She had never even thanked him for that.

And then of course, two years after returning to modelling, the e-mails started. The secret e-mails! The anger within him was now at boiling point, but he realised that he had to keep it under control. He sat up and poured himself another dose of medicine...a Glenmorangie, hoping that it might help him get some sleep that night.

It didn't, as it turned out. He didn't sleep a wink!

Chapter 71

It was 8-30 on Sunday morning and David was already showered and dressed. Amazingly he felt refreshed both physically and mentally, even although he hadn't slept well. He put it down to the fact that he had a clear picture in his mind of how he should handle this situation that he now found himself in, and he was determined to start the rest of his life from that very day.

Firstly, he would contact Gilberto and find out if there were any new developments, and as Gilberto had already treated him to a nice meal earlier that week, he decided to invite him out to dinner the following evening, to return the compliment.

Secondly he would continue searching for Louise both during the day and night, even although he now didn't expect to find her. The only difference being that he would take the Glock 17 with him during his night searches. He would also make sure that hotel staff knew that he was leaving the hotel to look for his wife. He had to put on a show that he was the distraught husband desperately searching for his missing loved one.

Thirdly he would book a flight home on Thursday, October 15th. The airline had told him that because of his predicament, they would fly him home anytime he wanted. He only had to ask. That time had come.

Next, he would telephone his boss and tell him he would return to work on Monday, October 19th. He had to try and get back to some kind of normal life, and he also needed the money to fulfil the next part of his plan. He would return once a month to the city of Barcelona, and he would make sure that Gilberto, Officer Villa, and everyone else involved in the case, knew the reason why he was there....to search for his beloved wife, unless she turned up before then. But he knew within himself that she wouldn't.

After he had booked his flight, spoken to his boss, and arranged his 'dinner date' with Gilberto, David went back out onto the streets of Barcelona, but not before he had stopped at reception to speak to Alfonso, who was stationed there that day.

"Good morning Alfonso, how are you today?"

"I'm fine sir. How about you? Do you have any news on your wife?"

"Not a thing, but I'm not giving up. That's where I'm going just now. I'm going to search for her again. Wish me luck!"

"Good luck sir" replied Alfonso before adding "and thank you very much for not mentioning my name to Assistant Chief Ramirez. Maria told me what you said."

"No problem Alfonso. I am a man of my word."

As David walked out of the hotel, Alfonso Pique was a relieved man, knowing that his name hadn't been brought up during the conversation in the restaurant the other evening. As he watched him disappear, Alfonso couldn't help but think that as well as being a very honest man, David Telfer was also a very devoted husband.

And that is exactly what David wanted him to think.

Chapter 72

David didn't search for long that day. After a few hours, he found a nice eatery and had himself a lovely lunch. He then returned to the hotel and had a few hours sleep before showering and changing his clothes for his night time patrol. The one thing that David had learned was that he should dress the same as the locals. Blend in.

"Do not dress like a tourist!" Maria had advised him. It was good advice.

The only difference this time was that he was packing a gun, a Glock 17, which he concealed in his inside jacket pocket. He didn't think many of the locals would be carrying one of those!

That day and night had been completely uneventful. He walked the streets hoping that one of those bastards who had given him a kicking would turn up and try it again, but it was not to be, and he eventually returned to his hotel at two o'clock in the morning, dead beat. He hoped that the following day might prove to be more productive. That night he had no problem getting to sleep. He was much more relaxed now, knowing his course of action.

Next day was more of the same, apart from the fact that he had to meet Gilberto for dinner at eight o'clock that Monday evening. So he finished his walkabout at about 6 pm and then changed for dinner, and walked over to Luigi's at about ten to eight. Surprisingly, Gilberto was already there, seated at the same table as their previous visit. He was also being served by the same waiter, Enrique.

"Good evening Gilberto, you look as if you have had a bad day!"

"I've had a horrendous day, and by the look of you, you haven't had the greatest of days either. Take a seat, I've already ordered the wine" answered Gilberto.

"You're very observant, I'm totally pissed off. I'm just not getting anywhere. Do you have any news that might cheer me up?"

"I'm afraid not, David, we keep hitting dead ends. It looks as though your wife has disappeared off the face of the earth, and we don't have one single witness!"

David shook his head, took a sip of his wine, and started to eat his pizza, which Enrique had just placed in front of him.

The two men sat in silence for a few moments before Gilberto completely changed the subject of the conversation.

"Do you like football?"

David was quite surprised, but at the same time he was relieved that Gilberto wanted to talk about something else other than the case of his missing wife, Louise.

"Yes I do, and I love to watch your team, Barcelona. I take it that you do support Barcelona?"

"Yes, they are my team, the best team in the world!" answered Gilberto.

That was it! For the next two hours they spoke about all the sports they enjoyed watching, although they talked mostly about football, and the obscene wages that the top players earned. They discussed their home towns, their upbringing, their families, and of course their wives. It was more like a bonding session than an off the cuff meal, because they seemed to agree in so many things. And of course there was the ultimate bond between them. They both lost their wives on the same day....Tuesday September 15th. That was a date that neither of them would ever forget.

Two bottles of wine later, and they were each on their last glass, when David started to tell Gilberto that he was going back home to Scotland. He explained how he felt, and that how he was now beginning to feel that there was nothing else he could do. He told him he had already contacted his boss to tell him when he would be returning to work, and that he was going to try and get some normality back into his life. But he emphasised to him that he would be back in Barcelona as soon as he could gather enough money together, and until such times he would be in contact every week to find out if there had been any new developments. He finished by saying that he would like to meet up with Gilberto again, when he returned, adding that he would like to try and repay all of his hard work on the case, by buying him tickets for a Barcelona match.

"You will do no such thing, David. In fact, I would be delighted if you would go to Saturday night's game against Athletico Madrid with me, as my guest. It will be a great game."

David thought to himself for a few moments before answering.

'Would it look bad if he was seen going to a football match while his wife was still missing?

Would it look bad if he was seen to be enjoying himself?

Would it look bad if he was seen in the company of the Assistant Chief of Police at the Barcelona match?'

He decided not...in fact it might be good for him, take his mind of his problems for a few hours.

"That would be great Gilberto. I've always wanted to see a game at the Camp Nou!"

"Bueno! I'll meet you here at 5 o'clock and we will have dinner first. See you then."

Both men stood up and shook hands before David turned and left Luigi's to turn in for the night. He had actually enjoyed his evening. But just as he made his way through the door he heard Gilberto ordering another bottle of wine. He turned around, looked at Gilberto and thought to himself that he (Gilberto) really was a very lonely man...... he missed his wife terribly.

Gilberto noticed David looking over, so he waved goodbye to him, and watched him leave the restaurant and cross the road to the hotel. When he finally saw David disappear through the hotel doors, he lifted his mobile phone, dialled the magic number and waited for an answer.

Seconds later he uttered the words, "David Telfer is leaving Barcelona next Thursday."

He then hung up, conversation finished!

Chapter 73

Not a lot had happened in the following ten days. David had walked the streets of Barcelona every night, apart from Saturday, including the seedier parts, with their peep shows and brothels, but no one had recognised the photograph of Louise. These were dangerous streets so he had taken the Glock 17 with him but had never had to use it.

There was only one time that he had felt threatened. Two drunks had come out of a brothel just as he had been showing the picture of Louise to some of the working girls who were standing on the street outside. They immediately started shouting abuse at David and followed him down the road. David prepared himself for trouble by unzipping his inside pocket and slipping his hand inside to grasp the gun. He grabbed it tightly and turned around to face the troublemakers. However just as he did so, they disappeared into a small bar which seemed to be filled with men of the same ilk.

Pressure off!

Apart from that incident, nothing else had happened. He hadn't found anyone who had recognised Louise, and Gilberto had no new developments to report either. His searches had all been a complete waste of time.

However, although he still felt slightly guilty, he had loved every minute of his Saturday night at the Barcelona match with Gilberto. Gilberto had managed to acquire great seats on the half way line, with a fantastic view of the pitch. It had been everything that David had ever imagined, and with Barca winning 3-1 the atmosphere had been electric from the start, with the one hundred and twenty thousand crowd continually shouting "Barca...Barca... Barca!"

David had constantly thanked Gilberto throughout the whole night for providing him with such a great experience, and had repeated again and again, that he didn't only regard him as the police officer who had helped him try to find his wife, but he regarded him from now on as a good friend. David remembered that Gilberto had become a little emotional when he had said this for the first time.

'Gilberto was indeed a very lonely and vulnerable man' he had thought to himself. 'That could make things a lot easier for me!'

And now here he was standing in reception that Thursday morning, waiting for his taxi to arrive to take him to the airport. He should have been back home with Louise by his side five weeks ago, but he now stood all alone, wondering what the future held for him without her. It was a very strange and emotional feeling, and yet he didn't feel like crying. Was there something wrong with him or was he just facing up to the stark reality of the situation he now found himself in? He decided it was the latter of those two options.

He wasn't standing alone for long, as Maria soon joined him, telling him that whenever he was going to return, he should phone the hotel and ask for her. She would use her hotel staff discount card to book him a room at a special price.

"Maria, I just can't thank you enough. I don't know what I would have done without you this last month. I hope you don't mind if I keep in touch with you, and maybe you could keep me up to date if anything crops up regarding Louise....anything at all, even the slightest scrap of information."

"I'm glad you said that, David, because I was going to suggest the same thing. You know I will help you in any way that I can."

They had already exchanged telephone numbers when David had returned the Glock to Maria the previous evening. He had waited until she had finished her shift, so that she could take it straight out of the hotel without anyone seeing it. They stood in the foyer looking at each other and the realisation hit them both that there was nothing else left to say, except goodbye. David's taxi ground to a halt outside of that huge hotel window, where he last saw Louise walking towards the bakery, and it was finally time for him to leave.

He lifted his case and kissed Maria on both cheeks.

"Thanks for everything, Maria. I'll be in touch soon. Adios."

"Adios David, I'm just sorry that I couldn't do more to help you find Louise."

"You did more than enough, thanks again. I will see you soon."

Outside, the taxi driver opened the back door of his car for David. He slid his case across the back seat, and then he positioned himself right next to the window. He waved to Maria as the taxi gently pulled away from the kerb. As she watched him disappear into the distance, she wiped a tear away from her eye with her snow white handkerchief, but she knew for sure that he would return one day. She would definitely see David Telfer again.

The Final Part

Chapter 74

There was one person that David had completely forgotten about, Danielle, Louise's boss, so he decided to put that right immediately. It was Sunday afternoon, on his first weekend back home, and he reckoned that this would be as good a time as any to catch her at home. The phone rang about half a dozen times before Danielle answered it.

"Hello Danielle, it's David Telfer here, how are you keeping?"

"I'm fine thanks David, how are you?"

"I'm okay, thanks. Well I'm not really, that's why I'm calling you. It's Louise."

"What's wrong? Has something happened to her?"

"Well....... yes. She has disappeared."

"What do you mean, David? Disappeared?"

David then explained everything that had happened on their holiday to Barcelona, and finished by saying, "So you see, she obviously won't be at work, that's why I'm calling you."

"Oh I see David, but didn't Louise tell you?"

"Tell me what Danielle?"

"Louise stopped working for me three years ago. She wasn't turning up for work, or she was off on a week's holiday abroad somewhere. I thought you knew."

David was taken aback. He knew not to expect the expected from Louise, but this WAS a surprise. However as he took it all in, it really did fall into place in the overall big picture.

He stuttered slightly, "Well eh......... I have to go now, Danielle. It's been nice speaking to you."

"Okay David, bye, and I hope everything works out alright for you, and you find Louise."

"I hope so, Danielle. Goodbye."

Monday morning and David was back at his work. His boss Sandy had asked him to go in a little earlier as he had wanted a little chat with him, to find out if indeed he seemed in the right frame of mind to start working again. He was in no doubt, David was fine, and he knew from the past, that he was a strong character.

David had already started planning for the future when he arrived home the previous week. He had already made an appointment with the bank manager, Mr Woods, as he wanted to ask him a few questions. He knew that he had to deal with certain things and get himself organised, and he might as well start as soon as possible. There was also one thing that he wanted to find out and the bank manager was probably the only one who could tell him.

That appointment was today at half past four, as soon as he finished work.

David arrived at the bank dead on time, and Mr Woods was waiting in his office, which was decorated with dark brown panelled wood on the walls and ceiling. Mr Woods sat behind a huge dark brown wooden desk. It was all very dull, probably just like Mr Woods, thought David as he was greeted by a tall pale faced man who seemed very sullen.

"Good afternoon Mr Telfer, how can I help you?"

"Hello Mr Woods, I just wanted to inform you of a change in my circumstances, and to ask you a few questions."

"Fire away!" answered the bank manager.

"Well, the fact of the matter is that my wife Louise has disappeared."

"What do you mean? Disappeared?"

"We were on holiday in Barcelona last month, and she simply disappeared. The police thought at first that she was the victim of an express kidnapping, but now they really don't know what to think."

"And what do YOU think, Mr Telfer?"

"To be honest I no longer know what to think! All I know is that I need to try and just get on with my life in the meantime, and hope that she turns up again, just as suddenly as she disappeared."

"And so, how can I help you Mr Telfer?"

"Well, first of all, we have a joint bank account. The fact that she has disappeared doesn't alter that in anyway, does it? I mean, if my wife has been kidnapped and somehow she escapes from her captors and needs money, she still will be able to access that account, won't she?"

"Certainly, that won't be a problem."

"The other question that I need to ask you is about the account that she had in her own name."

"I'm sorry Mr Telfer, but I can't give you any information about your wife's personal account without her say-so."

"But these are exceptional circumstances, Mr Woods, don't you agree?"

"Yes I do agree, but I still can't tell you anything about someone else's account without their permission."

"But I'm worried about my wife. She WILL still be able to access that account, no matter what?"

"Yes, off course. Look Mr Telfer, I'm sorry but I really can't discuss your wife's account without her permission."

"Can I ask you one last question, and then I won't ask you anything else?"

"Go ahead."

"Obviously, I'm extremely worried about my wife, and I just want to satisfy myself that wherever she is, at least she won't have any problems gaining access to money. So could you tell me if that account is still open?"

"Certainly, I can tell you that much."

Mr Woods started flicking his fingers out at his key pad, and seconds later the screen came to life. He asked David to repeat his wife's name and address, and then fed the details into his laptop.

David watched as the look of sheer surprise spread across the face of the glum looking bank manager.

"I'm sorry to have to tell you this Mr Telfer, but your wife no longer has an account with us. That account was closed last month."

"What date?" David immediately enquired.

"Thursday, September third."

David stood and stretched his right hand across the desk and shook Mr Woods's hand.

"Thank you very much, Mr Woods, you have been very helpful."

He then turned and walked straight out of the bank.

He wasn't in the least surprised at the news, as it was only what he expected. He just wanted it clarified.

Chapter 75

For one whole year David returned to Barcelona, once a month to search for his wife Louise. He made sure that everyone involved in the case knew why he was back, and after all of that time searching, they all respected him and regarded him as a devoted loving husband. Maria had managed to get him fixed up every month with cheap rates for his room at the hotel, and all of the workers who worked on reception were now on first name terms with him. In fact, he now had great football debates with Alfonso, who supported Real Madrid, the arch rivals of Barcelona. David had become a bona fide Barcelona supporter, due to the fact that Gilberto had taken him to some more games at the Camp Nou. Gilberto, who was now a very good friend, had tried to help him as much as he could, but then again he could only do so much.

Even Officer Villa now thought of him as a decent god-fearing man who was lost without his wife.

Carlos Angel Martinez seemed to have just faded into the background, and was always on holiday these days. He had never returned to the race for Mayor, and indeed now, according to Maria, he had even stopped making impromptu visits to the hotel. She, for one, was very pleased about that. She was still as beautiful as the first day he had clapped eyes on her, in Barcelona, now eight years before, and he was indebted to her for all the help she had given him during his times of trouble. He hoped to repay her one day.

As for Louise, she had never been seen since that day, Tuesday September 15th the previous year, the day she had vanished.

David hoped that this would be thirteenth time lucky... the thirteenth month in a row that he had visited Barcelona. This time he had saved up enough money to stay for a week, but only because he didn't have to pay for the hotel. This time he had been invited to stay at Gilberto's home and he had gratefully accepted. This was an opportunity for him to work on the next step of his plan.

For that whole week, David seemed very down. He sat in Gilberto's house every night, drinking red wine, or vodka and diet coke. He didn't go out, not even to Luigi's, his favourite restaurant. He didn't visit the hotel to speak to Maria, Alfonso or any of the other staff whom he now considered to be his friends. He didn't search for Louise, and he hardly spoke to Gilberto.

This wasn't like him and Gilberto was worried. Not only was he worried about David, he was also under pressure himself, from Carlos. He had already received a phone call from him earlier that day.

"Gilberto, what the fuck do you think you are playing at, inviting David Telfer to stay at your home? I've already told you to get rid of him. He keeps going back to the Hotel Sants, and reminding guests that his wife was kidnapped from my hotel. That's not very good for my business. So, if you don't do anything about it, I will. Now, get rid of him!"

Gilberto now found himself in a terrible position, between a rock and a hard place. On the one hand, he had become very friendly with David, and he wanted to help him. But on the other hand, he owed a lot to Carlos Angel Martinez, so he didn't want to upset him either. He had to come up with a solution to suit both of them.

The night before David was due to return to Scotland, Gilberto took a few bottles of wine home and ordered a takeaway meal from Luigi's. He was sure that

David would enjoy that, and he hoped that he could get him to talk about his problems, and reveal his true feelings.

It didn't take David long to open up. He had been drinking vodka all day while Gilberto had been at work, and after just one glass of wine, he broke down in tears.

"Gilberto, I can't go on like this. I miss Louise so much. I've walked the streets of Barcelona for the past year, and all for nothing. I'm getting nowhere. Your entire police force can't find one single witness who saw her. How the fuck can such a thing happen? If only I knew she was safe, I would feel a bit better. If only I knew that she wasn't being tortured in some dirty brothel, being forced to do things that she didn't want to do, then I would feel a bit better. I don't even know if she is dead or alive. As it is, I'm in no man's land. I'm the one who is being tortured!"

"Well, what is it you want David?"

"I want closure Gilberto. If she IS dead, I would rather know now. I haven't told you Gilberto, but I have lost my job and I have no money left. I can't keep up the mortgage payments on my house, so I'm going to lose that too. When I tell them that my wife is missing, it doesn't make any difference. They don't care. They only ask, 'is she dead?' Do you have a death certificate? I tell them she isn't dead, and they actually answer, 'that's a pity. If you had a death certificate your house would be paid off for you.' Gilberto, what kind of world do we live in, when a house seems to be worth more than life itself." David started to sob uncontrollably.

"David, they are only doing their job. Under law, someone who is missing cannot be pronounced dead until after they have been missing for five years. Until that term has passed I'm afraid that there is nothing you can do. That is how Louise will be referred to...Missing. "

"I won't last five years, Gilberto. In fact I DON'T WANT to last five years without knowing what happened to Louise. I need an end to this, one way or another!"

David then got up and went to bed, still crying. Gilberto felt very guilty about the whole affair and decided to try and sort it all out. He would attempt to fix it, so that everyone could get on with their lives, and start afresh, especially David Telfer.

That's why they called him the Fixer.

Chapter 76

Two weeks later and David was at his work, when he received a call on his mobile. (He had lied to Gilberto about losing his job). He asked his client if he could be excused for a minute, and he walked outside.

"Hello David, its Gilberto here. How are you?" asked Gilberto in a sombre voice.

"Not too good Gilberto, I'm in bed."

"But it's only three o'clock in the afternoon over there!"

"I know but I don't have any thing to get up for" answered David.

"Well I'm sorry David, but I have some news for you, and it might be bad, we don't know for sure yet."

David felt a bolt of electricity surge through his whole body.

"What is it? Is it Louise?"

"We're not sure. All I can tell you that a body has been found in a burnt out brothel in the back streets of Barcelona. We have received an anonymous tip off that it may be Louise, but I'm afraid we can't identify her, as the body is so badly burned. I'm sorry to have to ask you this, but could you ask her dentist to e-mail me her dental records so that we can make a definite identification. Is that possible?"

"Yes, of course it's possible! But what makes you think it might be Louise?" asked David in a shaking high pitched voice.

"One of the other girls who worked there, described your Louise perfectly. She told us that this lady had been working in the brothel for just over a year, which fits into the time scale. She also told us that the lady who died was a drug addict. I'm afraid this also fits in with the whole kidnapping scenario. As I told you at the time, there was a possibility that Louise might be sold into the sex trade, if they didn't get any ransom money. When they take this route they normally feed them with all sorts of drugs, and as they usually end up dependant on them, that's how the bastards control the women. Well, I'm sorry to have to say this to you David, but I'm afraid it looks as if that's exactly what happened in this case."

Gilberto paused for a moment then asked, "David, are you alright?"

David didn't know what to say. He stood in silence for a few moments, took several deep breaths and then answered Gilberto. "I'm okay. I'll get onto it right away."

David didn't know whether to laugh or cry. He had waited for over a year to reach this stage of his plan, so he didn't want to waste any more time. He immediately phoned Louise's dentist and put in his request. He obviously explained the situation to Mr Fallon, and gave him Gilberto's e-mail address.

He had started the wheels in motion for the next part of his master plan.

Chapter 77

Two nights later, as David made his evening meal, a meal for one, the telephone rang. It was a strange feeling, but he knew that it was Gilberto Ramirez. David picked up the receiver, knowing that the voice on the other end of the line would be his.

"Hello, David Telfer speaking."

"Buenas noches David, it's Gilberto here. We have definite results as to the identity of the body found in the brothel."

He paused for a second, to allow David to ready himself.

"I'm afraid it's Louise."

Gilberto couldn't hear a sound from the other end of the line.

And then David spoke.

"Are you sure? There's no doubt?"

"There's no doubt. I'm so sorry." Gilberto waited for a few moments to let the news sink in, and then asked, "Do you want to come over to Barcelona, or do you want me to arrange things from this side? I mean, do you want me to arrange to fly your wife's remains home to you?"

David couldn't think straight. He had waited all of this time for this moment, and now that it had finally arrived, he didn't know what to do. He started to cry.

"Hello David, are you still there?"

"Yes, I'm sorry Gilberto," said David in between sobs. "I just don't know what to do. What do you think?"

Gilberto could hear David crying and immediately decided what he should do.

"I think you should leave it all to me. You've suffered enough. I don't think you could take it, coming over here to collect the remains of your lovely wife. I will arrange everything and then contact you to let you know what's happening."

"Thank you so much Gilberto, how can I ever repay you?"

"Look David, don't you worry about anything. All I need you to do is to fax or e-mail me a copy of your travel insurance policy and I will do the rest. If you don't have a copy available, just let me know the name of the company you used and I will contact them myself. I'm sorry to have to ask you for such details but I'm afraid it can't be helped. After I get everything sorted out over here, all you will have to worry about is collecting your wife at your side, and then giving her a proper burial. The Barcelona coroner will send the death certificate directly to you within the next day or two, and you can start to arrange the funeral. Hopefully, after that you will be able to live your own life. You will have closure. Goodnight David. Try and get a good night's sleep, and hopefully I will be in touch soon, with all the arrangements."

David said goodnight, hung up the phone and went and took a beer from the fridge.

Chapter 78

It was seven o'clock in the morning and David was already awake, his mind awash with all the things he had to do. He hadn't realised how much organisation surrounded a funeral. But he still couldn't do much without a body or a death certificate. He decided to put his time to good use and start letting people know that Louise was dead. But he didn't want a big funeral. He would have preferred it if he was the only one in attendance. So he pondered over who he would contact while he ate his breakfast of bacon on toast. He finally came to the decision that he would get in touch with three people.

Firstly, Danielle, Louise's former boss and good friend.

Secondly, he would have to phone his own boss, Sandy, because he would have to let him know that he would be off work for a few weeks.

And thirdly, he would have to make contact with Gerry Black, Louise's father.

He decided to phone Danielle first. He waited until mid morning and then hesitantly lifted the phone. Someone picked up on the fourth ring.

"Good morning, is that you Danielle?"

"No I'm sorry its not, I'll just get her for you. Who shall I say is calling?"

It was a man's voice, so David assumed that it was her husband, although he realised that he didn't even know if she was married.

"Tell her that it's David Telfer please."

He could hear the man shouting at the other end of the line. "Danielle, there's a David Telfer on the phone for you."

There was a few seconds silence before David could hear footsteps running across the wooden floor, rushing towards the telephone.

"David? Have they found Louise? Is she alright?"

He took several seconds to compose himself and then he replied.

"Yes they have, but I'm afraid it's bad news." There was silence for a second time and then he continued once again. "Louise is dead."

"Oh no David! I'm so sorry. When did you find out?"

David could hear Danielle crying as he told her how the Assistant Chief of Police had called to tell him that they had identified the body of a woman found in a brothel in Barcelona as being that of his wife Louise.

"But how can they be sure its Louise? Maybe they've made a mistake!" asked Danielle hopefully.

"No it's definitely Louise. Assistant Chief Ramirez asked me to send him Louise's dental records so that they could be one hundred per cent certain it was her. There's no doubt."

"What happens now David?"

"I'm just waiting for Louise's body to be flown home along with the death certificate. The Assistant Chief is organising that......he really has been a great help to me."

There was a moments silence before David continued,

"I'm sorry Danielle but I really don't want to talk about it. I'll call you again when I have made all the funeral arrangements. Speak to you soon, bye."

He didn't even place the phone back in its cradle. He immediately dialled his boss's number and had exactly the same conversation.

Two down, one to go! But this was the hard one. Gerry Black had never liked David. He didn't think he was good enough for his only daughter, Louise, and they hadn't spoken to each other for many years. But David thought that he had a right to know that his daughter was dead. And besides he had a plan for winning Gerry Black over, and it would begin with a visit to his home in Stirling.

Chapter 79

David drove into the driveway of Gerry's eight bedroom mansion on the outskirts of Stirling. Gerry's father had made millions in the Dutch diamond trade and had left it all to his only son Gerry in his last will and testament. He was now seventy five years of age and retired. He loved his Victorian home and had many happy memories of the fifty one years he had stayed there. However there was one overriding moment of sadness, when his wife Claire died. She was only twenty four years of age at the time, when she died of a brain hemorrhage.

It ran in her family....her older sister had suffered the same fate at just twenty five.

Gerry still didn't know how he came through those dark times, but he knew that he would never have survived if it had not been for his daughter Louise. She was only one year old at the time, and it was up to him to make sure that he stayed strong for her sake. He had brought her up on his own and as she grew up, he regarded her not only as his daughter but also his best friend. They had some great times together in that big house.

However things changed the day she said she was getting married to David Telfer. Gerry had never taken to David, as he thought he wasn't good enough or wealthy enough for his little angel. He didn't want her to marry him, but the real truth was that it wouldn't have mattered who Louise was marrying. Gerry couldn't face the fact that someone was taking away the only treasure he had left in the world. Louise had already moved out to live with David in Airdrie, but Gerry had always hoped that she would return one day and everything would be back to normal. They eventually married and he realised that things would never be the same again.

David Telfer had taken his daughter away from him.

After the wedding Gerry didn't have much contact with Louise and David, only an occasional phone call. As the years passed by, they just seemed to drift apart. In the end, they didn't even exchange birthday or Christmas cards. There were times when Gerry thought about lifting the phone and calling Louise, but he was very stubborn, just like his daughter, and he didn't want to make the first move. He didn't want to be seen as being weak.

It was a sad state of affairs, and David Telfer was just about to make things a whole lot worse for Gerry Black. He opened the door of his black Mazda T2 and walked across the pebbled pathway towards his front door. He stood on the bottom step and buttoned then unbuttoned his suit jacket. He was extremely nervous. He hadn't spoken to Gerry Black for twenty years and here he was about to tell him his daughter was dead. But he knew that he had to go through with it, because David had decided to move to another country to start a new life, and he wanted to make things right with Louise's father before he left. He also hoped that he could relieve Mr Black of some of his money by making him feel oh so guilty about all those years he had shunned Louise.

This was his first step on his way to achieving both of those goals.

Chapter 80

The housemaid answered the door. She was a middle aged lady, with red hair cut in a bob shaped style that made it curl under her chin on both sides. She was dressed in a smart navy blue uniform, and had a French maid type headdress perched on her head. She was quite heavily built, and David imagined that she was the type of woman who was 'always on a diet'.

"Good afternoon sir, how can I help you?"

"Can I speak to Mr Black please?"

"Come in sir, and I'll just go and get him."

She showed him into a small room and invited him to sit down on an immaculate brown coloured leather two seater couch.

The photographs were the first thing that David noticed.

It looked like a photographic diary of Louise's life, from childhood through her teens until the last one in which she was twenty years old. He knew that, because he had seen that photo before. It had been taken by a professional photographer, and had made up part of her first modelling portfolio. There must have been a dozen photographs in that small room, and Louise was in every single one of them. Looking at those pictures, David couldn't understand how a man, who obviously deeply loved his daughter, could allow such a rift to develop between them.

'He must have really hated me' he thought to himself, 'this is going to be even tougher than I thought'.

Just then Gerry Black appeared in the doorway. He looked in great shape for his age, with his upright stance and a full head of thick wavy hair. The only difference David could see was that his hair was now white instead of the jet black that it used to be. David immediately rose to his feet and greeted him, and offered his right hand at the same time. Gerry Black ignored it.

"Hello Mr Black, you must be wondering why I'm here" said David in his most sombre voice.

"Its Louise isn't it? What's happened to her? Is she ill?" questioned Mr Black, the sound of panic in his voice. He knew that David Telfer wouldn't be making a social call.

"I'm afraid I have some bad news for you." David swallowed hard as he struggled to get the words out.

"I don't know how to tell you this." He stopped for a second, before continuing. "You're right. It is Louise........ Louise is dead. I'm sorry Mr Black but your daughter is dead."

Gerry Black had only ever cried twice in his lifetime as far as he could remember.....firstly, when his wife died, and secondly, at the passing of his own mother. He was old fashioned in his ideas about life, and he considered it a sign of weakness in a man if he shed tears, especially in front of another person. He raised his right hand to his face and rubbed his eyes with his thumb and index finger, and at the same time lowered his head until his chin rested on his chest. He was trying to hide his tears. Then his body began to shake uncontrollably. He shuffled slowly forward and managed to sit himself down on the couch next to David. He couldn't speak.

David didn't know what to say or do.

He thought about reaching across to comfort him, by putting his right arm around him and giving him a gentle squeeze.

He thought about trying to say something inspirational to help him deal with his grief.

He thought about leaving the room, to allow him to deal with it on his own.

In the end he didn't do anything. He just sat there in complete silence.

After several minutes of excruciating quiet, Gerry finally broke his silence. He wiped the tears away from his face with his neatly folded handkerchief, and asked David,

"What happened? How did she die?"

David proceeded to tell him about Louise's depression problems and how they decided to go on holiday to celebrate her full recovery from the illness. He told him about the theft of their bag in Barcelona and how it seemed to effect Louise for the rest of the holiday.

"She acted very strangely for the remainder of our cruise, and then when we finally returned to Barcelona, she simply disappeared. She left the hotel to go to a bakers shop right next door....she loved their doughnuts....and she never returned. That's the last time I ever set eyes on Louise."

"When did this happen?" asked a shocked Gerry Black.

"That was thirteen months ago."

"Why has it taken you all this time to come and tell me?"

"Because Louise had disappeared before........during her illness. But she always came back. I really did believe that she would turn up. I walked the streets of Barcelona day and night searching for her, but she seemed to have just vanished off the face of the earth. The Assistant Chief of Police was put in charge of the case, but even with the resources he had at his disposal, he couldn't find Louise. After weeks of constant searching I had to return home. I went back every month to look for Louise and find out if there had been any developments....but there weren't any. Nothing."

"Why didn't you come to me for help? You know that I could've financed any kind of search, for any length of time!" Gerry asked disbelievingly.

"Well, we've never exactly been on speaking terms over the years Mr Black, and I really did think Louise would reappear...but I was wrong. And then two nights ago I received a phone call from the Assistant Chief of Police, Senor Gilberto Ramirez. That call confirmed my worst fears. They had found the badly burned body of a woman in a city centre building, and he told me that it was definitely Louise." David didn't want to tell him that it was a brothel.

"But how could he be so certain, if the body was so badly burned? How could he identify her?"

"He had already made contact with me, and had asked me to send him Louise's dental records. I'm so sorry but it's definitely Louise."

Gerry Black rose to his feet and walked over to the mantlepiece. There, he lovingly stroked one of the photographs of Louise with the back of the fingers of his right hand. He couldn't believe that his beautiful daughter was dead, and that he had missed so much of her life because he was so stubborn and pigheaded. And now it was too late to fix it!

"Gerry."

It was the first time that David had ever called him by his first name.

"I'm here for another reason. I need your permission to do something, and if you agree, I think it might help you deal with all of this. I know it will help me."

Gerry Black slowly turned round to face David Telfer, the man who had taken his angel from him. He couldn't think of one single thing that he could say or do that would make him feel better. He was heartbroken.

"I would like your permission to bury Louise beside her mum. I think she would have wanted that. I think you would like that."

Gerry couldn't believe what he was hearing. David Telfer was giving him his daughter back.

For years David had been hated by Gerry Black, but with those few words, he had instantly gained his utmost respect. Gerry realised how hard it must have been for David to come to his house that day, and give him that dreadful news, especially after the way he had been treated for all of those years. Gerry Black had ignored him for more than twenty years.

"Thank you David. I would like that. I would like that very much."

He then walked over to him and shook him warmly by the hand. They hugged each other for the first time in their lives. As they released each other from their grasps they both felt slightly uncomfortable.

"I have to go now Gerry....I'm waiting on a call from Assistant Chief Ramirez. He's going to tell me when I can expect Louise home. As soon as I find out the details I'll come back and see you. Maybe you can help me with the organisation of the funeral?"

"That won't be a problem David."

As David turned and walked towards the door, a broad smile spread across his face. This part of his plan was working out better than he had thought.

Chapter 81

The Funeral

Ten days later, David and Gerry found themselves at Edinburgh airport to collect the body of Louise, their beloved wife and daughter. The day after his visit to Gerry, David had received the dreaded call from Gilberto Ramirez giving him all the details about the return of her remains. He had already received the death certificate from the coroner, and so from that day, David and Gerry had worked together to organise Louise's funeral. They had arranged for the hearse and one limousine to travel to the airport and take the remains back to the undertakers. There the body, or what was left of it, would be placed in the coffin already chosen jointly by both of them, ready for the funeral which was to take place at Our Lady and St Ninians Church in Stirling the very next morning. There was only one problem. Assistant Chief Ramirez had warned David not to look in the coffin, but to picture Louise in his mind the way he wanted to remember her. He would never recognise the rickle of bones that once was his beautiful wife. David explained this to Gerry, and although he was desperate to see her again for one last time, he accepted that it was probably good advice, and didn't force the issue. He decided to settle for just getting her back.

St Ninians was a beautiful old church built in eighteen fifty one. It had been refurbished quite recently, but still retained all of its old fashioned charm. As David stood at the back of the chapel for the first time, on that cold but sunny November morning, he couldn't help but marvel at the beautiful scene before him. Below the crisscross wooden beams of the Tudor style high ceiling, the original four seat wooden benches ran along both sides of the outer walls from back to front, twenty five in all at each side. One aisle at each side separated them from the eight seater pews, which ran straight down the centre of the church. Above the altar at the front of the chapel, was a multi coloured stained glass window, which depicted the birth of Jesus in the stable in Bethlehem.

As David looked down the church, the sun's rays seemed to pierce the window like rainbow coloured lances, and embed themselves in Louise's beautiful oak coffin, which stood between the front pew and the marble altar.

It was a sight to behold. David was glad that he had decided to go to the church early that day, so that he could spend some time alone, gathering his thoughts and saying his personal prayers. It wasn't long before he was joined by Gerry Black, who sat beside him in the front seat, shoulder to shoulder.

At ten o'clock the funeral ceremony began, with only about fifty people in attendance. They were mostly from Gerry's side, acquaintances and long lost cousins, and a few of David and Louise's friends from many years before. The priest gave a beautiful sermon, and spoke about her lovingly, as he knew her very well as a child who regularly attended his masses. In fact he had baptised her in that very church. It was all very emotional, especially when he gave his final blessing, and asked God to accept Louise into heaven. He then gave the signal to the pall bearers to come forward and take her to her final resting place. It was just as he said this that David Telfer fell to his knees. Gerry grabbed him by the arm and hauled him back to his feet.

"Be strong David. Be strong. It's nearly over."

The organist then started to play the final hymn, and the congregation immediately joined in the singing.

'Walk with me o my Lord,
Through the darkest night and brightest day.
Be at my side oh Lord,
Hold my hand and guide me on my way.'

The four pall bearers started to walk down the aisle carrying the coffin shoulder high and David and Gerry took their rightful place immediately behind them. The rest of the mourners then fell in behind, as the procession slowly made its way to the waiting hearse, which was parked just outside the church. Gerry wrapped his left arm around David and supported him every step of the way. With the coffin safely in the hearse, they then made their way to the graveyard.

By the time they reached the grave, the weather had taken a turn for the worse. The bright November sun had disappeared, to be replaced by rain.......heavy rain. The priest and the mourners huddled together around the grave, under a host of different coloured umbrellas. He said several prayers and then gave a short final blessing, ending with the sign of the cross. David and Gerry waited until everyone had gone and then said their personal goodbyes to Louise.

Firstly, Gerry walked over and threw some dirt on top of the coffin, quietly said a prayer and turned and walked away. At least he had his daughter back, and he could come and speak to her and his wife anytime he wanted. He was as happy as he could possibly be amid all of this misery.

Then David found himself all alone at the graveside. He grabbed a handful of dirt from the little dish provided by the gravediggers, and threw it into the grave. He then said one Hail Mary, blessed himself and walked away.

David Telfer could now try and move on. He could try and get on with his own life again, now that Gilbert Ramirez had given him what he wanted.

He had given him his closure.

Chapter 82

Over the following weeks, David visited Gerry on a regular basis. In fact he moved in with him from mid-November until just after the start of the New Year. David's sales territory had changed and he now had to cover the Fife region, and the north east of Scotland. So when Gerry had suggested that he make his base in his home in Stirling, David was only too pleased to take up his invitation. They grew much closer and Gerry even took him to his local pub for his weekly Friday night get together with his friends. David knew that things were going exactly to plan, when on that first Friday pub night, Gerry introduced him to his friends.

"This is my Son in Law, David Telfer." He had never referred to him as his Son in Law before.

As for Gerry, he enjoyed David staying in his home. He enjoyed the stories that David told him about his life with Louise. He liked to hear about all the places they had been on holiday together, and about all the happy times thay had spent together. Gerry loved to ask David questions about Louise, and they sometimes stayed up to the early hours of the morning, talking about her. Gerry was learning things about his daughter that he thought he would never know.

He was happy.

David spent Christmas at Gerry's, and on Christmas night, they both even went to the local pub's Christmas party. They weren't really looking forward to it, but found that it actually helped them deal with their recent problems. Inevitably they returned home that night and spent many hours talking about Louise, and reminiscing about all the good times. It was a nice Christmas, better than either of them had expected.

He also brought in the New Year at Gerry's, and it was on New Year's night that he decided to tell Gerry of his future plans.

"Gerry, I've really enjoyed spending time with you, and I've loved staying in your beautiful home these past weeks. It's been great reminiscing about all the good times, and filling you in with some of the happy events in Louise's life.....I hope you enjoyed that as much as I did. That has helped me a lot. It has also helped that I've got to know you better, and I want to thank you for being so good to me, but the real truth is that I'm not dealing with things very well when I'm alone, so I have come to a decision. I want to start a new life somewhere else. I don't know where I'm eventually going to stay, but I've booked a flight to Dublin for Monday the 17th of January. I have a friend over there who has invited me over for a few days, so I have decided to go. I've already handed in my notice to my boss, and I've just sold my house...everything will be finalised next week. If you don't mind, I would like to stay here until then, as I've already put all my furniture into storage. Will that be okay?"

Gerry was geniuinely surprised. He thought David had been coping quite well.

"Sure it's ok, but won't you think about changing your mind?"

"I've thought long and hard about this Gerry, so I won't be changing my mind."

"I respect your decision David and I will support you whatever you want to do."

"Thanks again Gerry. I'll see you in the morning, goodnight."

David then went to bed, happy in the knowledge that he had told Gerry of his plans. He had deliberately given him a fortnight to think about it, hoping that at the end of it, he would come to the decision to give him a parting gift.

In the meantime he went to sleep that night pleased that it would only be two weeks before he could move on to the final part of his plan.

Chapter 83

Monday the 17th of January and David was leaving Gerry's house at six o clock in the morning to catch his flight. At least that's what he had told Gerry. The truth was that he was going to spend the night in a hotel and then catch his flight the next morning. Gerry had offered to drive him to the airport but David had declined, saying that he had to return his company car to his work and that he had already organised a lift into Glasgow airport.

Gerry was up early to see David off.

"I'm glad I finally got to know you David.......you're a nice guy. I'm only sorry that Louise had to die before I realised that I was so wrong. I'm so sorry! I want you to take this. This is as much for me as it is for you....the reason I'm giving you this. I want to help you with that fresh start that you want. Good luck."

He then handed a white envelope to David.

David tried to refuse but Gerry wouldn't hear of it. David thanked him, shook his hand, and then hugged him, before saying his goodbyes. He left Gerry standing on the top step and walked over to his car. As he drove out of the gates he opened the car window and shouted to Gerry,

"I'll be in touch! Thanks for everything."

Gerry just waved as the car disappeared out of his driveway.

The truth was that David Telfer never had any intention of getting back in touch with Gerry Black. He had what he wanted from him. He had a cheque for two hundred and fifty thousand pounds.

Guilt money!

Chapter 84

Tuesday the 18th of January and David was indeed on his way to Glasgow airport, but he wasn't going to Dublin, he was flying to Barcelona for the final time. It was going to be a one day stay.... in and out. He would do what he had to do, then leave. Everything was organised. He would be picked up at Barcelona airport, driven to where he had to go, do what he had to do, then leave the country. This was indeed the final leg of his plan, which had been formulated so long ago. When he had booked the flight for that Tuesday morning, he had phoned his contact in Barcelona. Everything was now in place. He had finished all of his business in Scotland. He had sold the house, packed his job in, and tied up all the loose ends. He was ready to go!

He arrived at Barcelona airport at 10-15 am, right on schedule. Ten minutes later he was sitting in the back of his contact's car, on his way to his final destination. It would take them approximately one hour to reach the house, just in time to see the gardener leave through the side gate on his way home for lunch. His contact had watched this house every Tuesday for the past ten months, and knew all the comings and goings for a Tuesday, every Tuesday in life. No staff worked on a Tuesday, apart from the gardener. No housemaids, no cooks, and the chauffeur always drove the man of the house to work that day. It was now the only day of the week that he worked.

Ten minutes to twelve, and they were sitting in the parked car one hundred yards down the road from the big house. Bang on noon, the side gate opened and the gardener walked out. He closed the gate behind him but didn't lock it, he never did, he would only be gone one hour.

It was time for action.

David left the car, walked down the street and in through the side gate. He knew that the main front door of the house would be locked, but he also knew that the back door would be open to allow the gardener access to the main house. His contact had done a good job. He slowly opened the back door and walked through the kitchens until he found himself standing in the main entrance area, looking up at a huge marble spiral staircase. He then slowly and deliberately climbed the stairs, making sure that he didn't make any unnecessary noises. At the top of the staircase he stopped, and looked down to the far side of the landing, and there was the door that his contact said would be there.

'It will be the door facing you when you reach the top of the stairs.'

David was nervous but he knew that everything had been meticulously planned, so nothing could go wrong. He walked towards the door and gently turned the handle with his latex gloved right hand. In the middle of the room, there stood a massive four poster bed with drapes hanging down each side. Someone was still lying in the bed, facing away from David, towards a huge bay window. Suddenly the bed covers moved and the person in the bed turned quickly around, asking at the same time, "Is that you Carlos?"

This was the moment that David had dreamed about for more than a year, and he was amazed to find that he felt so calm and in control now.

"Hello Louise. How are you keeping?"

Louise was absolutely stunned. She was so shocked. Shocked that David wasn't.

Chapter 85

It took Louise a few moments to regain her composure. David sat down in a comfy armchair which stood just inside the door while Louise pulled herself up to sit on the edge of the bed. As she sat there ashen-faced, she couldn't believe how calm and relaxed David looked as he sat there like a king on his regal throne.

"David, what are you doing here?"

"I'm here to see YOU. I want to keep you up to date with what's happening."

"How did you know I was here?"

"Contacts, Louise, contacts. I've known for the past ten months that you were living here. Well that is, when you're not gallivanting around various parts of the world on holiday. I just need to ask you some questions... the first one being WHY? Why did you do this to me?"

Louise thought for a moment and then answered.

"I did it because I love you."

David burst out laughing. "What the hell are you talking about Louise? Are you trying to be funny?"

"No! You don't understand. I met Carlos years ago, on a modelling assignment in Barcelona, and we became great friends. But it is only in the last three years that our relationship grew into something else...love. I made up my mind that I would leave you and join Carlos in Barcelona, but I didn't know how to do it. I didn't want to hurt you. I still need you David. You have always been there for me when things got bad. I needed you to be there in case things didn't work out with Carlos. I thought that if I simply walked away from you, you might never take me back. But if I was kidnapped, and someone actually took me away from you by force, if things didn't work out, you would welcome me back with open arms."

"You have a warped mind Louise! Did you never stop for a minute to consider my feelings in all of this? And just when you talk about the last three years, Danielle told me that you hadn't worked for her during that period. So I suppose you were jetting off to see Carlos when you told me you were going on modelling assignments?"

"I'm afraid so David, I'm so sorry! Carlos just booked everything, and paid for it, obviously. He also set up a bank account for me and paid money into it so that I didn't have to work."

"Oh, I knew about that account."

"How did you know about it?"

"Well, during the time when you were drinking quite heavily, you used to fall asleep, and on many occasions you left your bank account details on screen. So to be honest with you, for the last three years before you disappeared I started taking money from that account to pay the premiums for the insurance policy that I took out on you. Otherwise I could have never afforded it. Money is no problem to Carlos, is it? I know now that 'money' is what you really love Louise. Money and power, and Carlos had both in abundance. Our problems really began when the money ran out. I know that now. And then when you met Carlos I knew it was only a matter of time before you left me, but I didn't know when or where that would happen. So I've been preparing myself for this moment for the past four years now....ever since I discovered your secret e-mail address...loucam at yahoo.co.uk."

Louise's face turned even whiter. She had sent and received some intimate messages to and from that address.

"How did you know about that?"

"Same way as your bank account...you fell asleep and left it on screen. It was easy to guess your password. You always use the same one, 'brandy', the name of your pet dog when you were a kid. So I followed your secret relationship for the three years before your 'kidnapping', and I knew it was coming to a head after you received your last message just before we left on holiday. Can you remember it?

Won't be long now, and we will be together for ever,
We will never be apart again
Love Cam xxx

Awwww, that's lovely, don't you think?" said David sarcastically, leaning his head to one side as he said it.

"David, I don't know what to say. What do you want me to say?"

"I don't want you to say a fucking thing. Just sit there and answer my questions when I ask. Okay?"

For the first time since David had walked into the room, Louise could see that he was losing his cool a little. She didn't want to upset him anymore, so she just sat there and did what she was told.

Chapter 86

David quickly regained his composure, as he straightened himself up in his chair.

"I'm sorry for swearing, Louise, but sometimes you just drag it out of me! Next question... why were you so cruel to me on the cruise ship?"

"I was trying to make you so angry that when I actually disappeared, you wouldn't feel so bad. You would still be angry at me."

"That's not a good answer, but you know what? I don't care. Next question! Was Carlos on board staying on deck 17, and did you visit him there?"

"Yes, he was, and I did. That's where I had been, the day you met me coming out of the lift."

"I knew it!" shouted David as he punched the air with his right fist. "And did he follow us that day, when we took the bus trip to Mdina?"

"He didn't follow us, but he was on the same trip."

David nodded his head. "That's the day I felt we were being watched! We were....by him!"

He paused for a moment and then asked his next question.

"Did you deliberately push me onto the road in Naples, and try to kill me?"

"Of course I didn't try to kill you! There were such a lot of people crowding around the kerbside that day, I don't know what happened. I was just so happy that you weren't badly hurt."

"Talking of killing people, why did three people have to die?"

"That wasn't meant to happen. When we planned it, it seemed so straightforward."

"Who planned it?"

"Carlos and I planned it together. I was simply to disappear and Gilberto Ramirez, the Assistant Chief, who works for Carlos, was supposed to sweep everything under the carpet. You would go home and that would be the end of it."

"And had you met Gilberto before that day our bag was stolen?" asked David.

"Yes I'd met him several times when I had visited Barcelona to meet up with Carlos."

"I knew it!" answered David. "And what made you change that simple plan?"

"Emilio Torres started blabbing off to his uncle, Juan Marquez, and Gilberto had to kill him to keep him quiet. He tampered with the brakes of his car, and he and the young man who had hired him to steal our bag, Eduardo Salgado, were both killed in that 'accident'. Gilberto was frightened that he would be dismissed from his job in disgrace, if anyone found out that he had set up a bag theft. As for Juan Marquez, he was trying to blackmail Carlos. He had taken a photograph of Carlos and me in one of the hotel rooms, the Saturday night before we left on the cruise."

"So that was you in that photo?"

"Yes, I was wearing a long black wig so that I wouldn't be recognised going into that room. He faxed a copy of that picture to Carlos and asked him for one million euros. Carlos couldn't stand for that, so he told Gilberto to fix it. He did so, by pushing him over his balcony. David I'm so sorry, none of this was meant to happen."

"But it did, and it was your fault. Do you know what I went through? I was arrested, locked up and beaten by that Officer Villa. He put me through sheer hell. And then I walked the streets of Barcelona searching for you, and I was beaten up again, by two thugs."

"Yes, I know all of that."

"YOU KNEW! And you stood by and watched from afar. You could have stopped all of this at any time. You just had to show yourself. For fuck sake Louise, I could have been killed."

David stopped talking for a few minutes rubbed his forehead with his right hand and once again straightened himself up on his chair. Moments later he asked,

"How did you stage your disappearance?"

"That was the simple part. You remember when I went to get a doughnut? Well just before I left I called Carlos and told him that I was leaving. If you can remember, he arrived just after that, in his Jaguar. When the chauffeur dropped him off, he just drove off further down the street, and I got into the back of the car. As it had black tinted windows, no one could see me. Carlos came out of the hotel and we drove to this house. Simple! That's the day you spoke to him."

"Yes, and that's when I knew something was going to happen...especially when he introduced himself to me as Carlos Angel Martinez ---CAM--- the abbreviation in your e-mail. Why did he stop his campaign to become Mayor of Barcelona?"

"He stopped because the whole 'mayor thing' was attracting too much publicity. We just wanted to be together, and he had arranged for us to go on a month's holiday immediately after my disappearance, to get away from it all. After that he decided not only to withdraw from the race for Mayor, but also to take a step back from all of his business interests. That's why he only works one day a week now. He just wanted to fade into the background so that we could live in peace and quiet. We love each other."

"You don't love Carlos, Louise, you love his money! And tell me, how did you manage to go on holiday with him, when you didn't have a passport? You left your passport in your bag when you disappeared!"

"The passport I left in the bag was a copy. Carlos had that one made. I took the real one out of the bag just before I left you."

"You certainly had it well planned Louise, I'll give you that much. But the one thing that you didn't count on was that I was onto you. I knew you were up to something, and it was only a matter of time before I found out about your sneaky little plan, and came back to get you. That time is now!"

Chapter 87

"Do you want to know what I've been doing for the past fifteen months, Louise?" asked David. The calmness had returned to his voice.

"Yes, I would David. I know that you have been coming to Barcelona every month for the past year to look for me. That was very nice of you David, it shows that you still love me."

David couldn't believe what he was hearing. Was she trying to rile him up, or was she being serious? He didn't know what to think, but he wasn't going to lose his temper now. He was in control of this situation.

"Yes, as you say, I've been coming to Barcelona every month for the past year, but not to look for you. I was PRETENDING to look for you. There's a big difference."

"What do you mean, pretending to look for me?"

"I wanted everyone to think that I was the distraught, devoted, loving husband who would do anything to get his wife back. But nothing could be further from the truth. I wanted to give everyone that impression. But most importantly, I returned here to make friends with Assistant Chief Gilberto Ramirez. I was very, very lucky in that department. His wife died the same day that you disappeared, and that provided a real link, a bond between the two of us that made my job so much easier. He took me to football matches, we ate out together and we became friends....he even let me stay at his house on my last visit. But I was only using him. I knew that he felt sorry for me, but at the end of the day he still worked for Carlos Angel Martinez, and HE wanted me out of Barcelona for good.

Deep down Gilberto really wanted to help me, because he felt so guilty. He had known from the start what was happening, and although he didn't like it, he had to go along with it. He knew where you were, right from the start, but he couldn't tell me, so on my last trip I planted a seed in his mind. An idea that he might take up, that would help both Carlos and me. I told him that I wanted closure and that I would only really be able to move on if I knew the truth... even if you were dead. I pretended to be losing it, and even suggested that I might end it all. That was it. Gilberto did the rest. That brings me to the last piece of news I have to tell you."

David took a deep breath before he continued.

"Gilberto found a body in a burnt out brothel in Barcelona, and he swapped your dental records with those of the dead woman. I didn't ask him to do it. I'm not even supposed to know what he did, but I do. That meant that the coroner could issue a death certificate...your death certificate. You are now dead and buried in the graveyard back home in Stirling. Your Dad even helped me organise the funeral."

"But my Dad hasn't spoken to you for years. You're a lying bastard."

"No I'm not Louise. I'm telling the truth. When I told him of your death, your Dad was in a terrible state, but when I gave him the opportunity to bury you, his only daughter, beside your Mum, his feelings changed towards me. In fact he even introduced me to his friends as his 'Son in Law'. Did you ever think that your Dad would ever refer to me as that?"

Louise shook her head in disbelief!

"No I didn't think so! However that's not all. He even gave me a cheque for two hundred and fifty thousand pounds to help me start my new life. I suppose you could call that my 'piece de resistance'.

Louise couldn't believe what she was hearing. Here was her husband David telling her that she was officially

dead! Not only that, but she had also had a funeral ceremony, was now buried in a graveyard in her hometown of
Stirling, and her scheming husband had conned her father
out of a quarter of a million pounds!

This was not working out the way she had planned.

"You look surprised Louise. I take it Carlos hasn't
told you about that part about the death certificate. It was
he who gave the go ahead to Gilberto to fix it. As you know
that's what he calls him, the Fixer."

Chapter 88

Forty five minutes had elapsed since David had entered the house, he had fifteen minutes left.

It was then that he heard a voice calling from downstairs. "David, watch your time!"

David looked at Louise and said, "I think you should meet my contact." He then turned, opened the bedroom door and shouted, "Come on up!"

While they waited, he explained about the other money he now had safely deposited in his bank account.... the £290,000 that he had received from the sale of their house, and the £750,000 from the payout from the insurance company after her death.

"Thanks for paying off the house Louise, and I really appreciate that insurance money. Combined with the money that your Dad gave me, that should help give us a good start somewhere. I never ever thought that I would have more than a million pounds in my bank account. Thank you, but it doesn't change the fact that you treated me like dirt for all of those years. I am due that money! You used me! You are one evil bastard for treating me that way."

Just at that the bedroom door slowly opened, and David stood up.

"Louise, I know you have already met, but I would like to introduce you formally. Louise, meet my new partner Maria Lopez, the hussy from the hotel."

David wrapped his left arm around Maria's waist and pulled her towards him. He kissed her fully on the mouth and fondled her left breast with his right hand.

This was a show for Louise.

Maria slowly moved her left hand down and seductively rubbed the top of David's thigh, and then his crotch. She loved it. She was telling Louise... 'He's mine now, all mine!'

"We've known each other for many years, since the first time I went to Barcelona eight years ago, and we have been seeing each other ever since!" said David when he came up for air.

"You bastard!" screamed Louise. "You are nothing but a fucking hypocrite!"

She jumped off the bed and ran towards the two of them. David gently pushed Maria to the side, grabbed Louise and lifted her off the ground as she tried to kick and punch him. He threw her back onto the bed, and signalled for Maria to leave the room by nodding his head to one side.

"Go and get changed Maria, I'll get you in the car." As for Louise, she continued to shout obscenities at both David and Maria.

"Calm down Louise, I'll be leaving in a minute. I have a flight to catch. There's only one last thing I have to do."

"And what's that David? Let me guess. Plead with me to come back with you? Not a chance! You're just a puny little man who I don't need anymore. So you can take your little hussy, and get out of my house, before I phone Carlos. So fuck off!"

"No. I'm afraid you're way off the mark with that one Louise. You remember that I said that you are now officially dead. Yes? Well no one can die twice, so I'm here to sort out that problem."

David then calmly pulled the Glock 17 from his pocket and shot Louise three times. He waited for a few minutes to make sure that she was definitely dead, and then turned and sauntered out of the room, before finally adding in his most sarcastic tone,

"Adios Louise, thanks for everything!"

Chapter 89

Three hours later and David Telfer and Maria Lopez were sitting in the departure lounge of Barcelona airport, waiting for their flight. Maria had changed into a short red skirt, red high heels, and a tight white blouse that accentuated her voluptuous curves. She also wore dark glasses that only added to her look, the look of a glamorous model. David couldn't believe his luck. He was sitting with over a million pounds in the bank, and a beautiful sexy lady on his arm, all thanks to his twice dead wife Louise. As for Maria she had finally found her Don Juan, her knight in shining armour, who was about to fly her off to the other side of the world...just what she had always wanted. They sipped pina colada cocktails as they waited for the announcement of their flight departure.

Two minutes later, their wait was over.

"Would passengers travelling to Rio on flight number TAP 743, please make their way to gate number seven."

"My lucky number" said David, as he put on his shades.

They then both stood up, chinked their glasses together, and said simultaneously,

"Here's to a new life!"

They sat their empty glasses down on the table, hugged, and then kissed each other passionately, before heading off to gate number seven.

No one has seen David Telfer or Maria Lopez since that day!

The End

20623952R00160

Made in the USA
Charleston, SC
20 July 2013